The Pirates of "the Foam"

Vol. II

SALZWASSER
VERLAG

C.F. Armstrong

The Pirates of "the Foam"

Vol. II

Reprint of the original, first published in 1863.

1st Edition 2022 | ISBN: 978-3-37500-252-7

Verlag (Publisher): Salzwasser Verlag GmbH, Zeilweg 44, 60439 Frankfurt, Deutschland
Vertretungsberechtigt (Authorized to represent): E. Roepke, Zeilweg 44, 60439 Frankfurt, Deutschland
Druck (Print): Books on Demand GmbH, In de Tarpen 42, 22848 Norderstedt, Deutschland

THE

PIRATES OF "THE FOAM."

A NOVEL.

BY

C. F. ARMSTRONG, Esq.

IN THREE VOLUMES.

VOL. II.

London

1863.

THE PIRATES OF THE FOAM.

CHAPTER I.

A LONG tropical day was drawing to its close, the sun was approaching its setting. In a few minutes it would be lost to sight in the bright glistening waters. The stillness of the lagoon and its placid surface, became gently rippled by the evening breeze then rustling before the still leaves of the forest, and various sounds were heard amid its dark recesses, betokening the awakening to life of the various denizens, who, during the day, rarely move.

It was sun-set, and Arthur Bolton and his

young companion were still buried in a deep sleep. Just at this period three canoes came paddling up to the lagoon from the westward. Now this sheet of water had a direct communication with the broad stream of the Punza Pulka river, where the unfortunate brig, the "Foam," lay a-ground, by a narrow and in parts by a very rapid stream. In the leading canoe were six Sambo Indians; in the other Bill Saunders and the Mexican desperadoes. Driven from plundering the "Foam," by the unexpected appearance of the "Maria Gloriosa," they had pulled up the river into the creek, and then made their way to the Sambo village of Quamwatta, the inhabitants of which were the most ferocious and brutal of the race.

The canoe containing our unfortunate heroine and her devoted attendant had been urged up another creek, which would take them direct to Quamwatta, where they were consigned by Saunders to the care of a party of Sambos, whilst he and his desperats associates towed their canoes through the creek into the inner lagoon, their purpose being to seek for the very men and the vessel from which our hero and Joe had so narrowly escaped with their lives.

As the canoes approached the shore, one of the Mexicans said to Will Saunders, "There's the hut," pointing to the one in which our hero slept, quite unconscious of the near approach of his most deadly enemy;

"Come, then," returned Saunders, "we will go in and wait till your comrades land from the schooner; with their help we will manage yet to have the gold out of the brig; we'll scuttle her, by means of Iose, the diver, sooner than let the 'Guarda Costa' carry her off as a prize."

Here the Sambos in the first canoe, after a few words with the Mexicans, pulled across to the opposite side of the lagoon, whilst Saunders and his four associates grounded their canoes just upon the spot where the Indian girl had started from some hours before, and where, notwithstanding the sounds of the men's voices, our hero and Joe slept.

Stepping out of the canoe, they pulled her up, took out a large kind of mat basket, full of provisions, and then they all walked up to the hut, against which were piled large heaps of dried wood. Two of the Mexicans spoke broken English, and Saunders, who had been an adventurer on that coast before, could speak a little Spanish.

"Why, here's a goodly collection of fire-wood," said Saunders; "who's been here?"

"Some of the cursed Woolwa Indians," returned one of the Mexicans; "they often come to this part of the coast for turtle."

By this time the sun had set, and twilight there is none, therefore, when Saunders advanced, before striking a light to examine the hut, it was quite dark.

So singularly sound did Arthur and Joe sleep, that not till Saunders gave a shout of exultation, when the light from the dry piece of wood he held flashed on their upturned faces, did they awake.

The villain had recognized them at once. Starting up at the sound of his voice, Arthur at once saw his foe, whilst Joe lay shaking with terror, thinking it must be some frightful dream.

"So here you are!" exclaimed Saunders.

Arthur stood ready prepared for a deadly struggle, Saunders having drawn his long Mexican knife.

"Come out, Saunders, quick, quick!" exclaimed the Mexicans outside the hut. "Here's three canoes full of Woolwa Indians; our deadly enemies."

"Not," returned Saunders, with a frightful imprecation, "till I have dug this beggar's eye out—an eye for an eye—" and, dropping the torch, he sprang at our hero; but Arthur warded off the blow, getting only a deep gash on the left arm, and caught his antagonist by the throat, and, after a frightful struggle, both rolled over on the floor.

Joe threw himself on Saunders's arm, grasping the hand that held the knife, and at that instant the hut became enveloped in flame.

Blinded and half suffocated by the smoke, the two powerful men relaxed their hold of each other, and rising, together with Joe, staggered out of the blazing hut in time to see the Mexicans, aided by the light of the flames which shewed all around them, and shone on the bosom of the lagoon, hastening towards the canoes.

The Indians in the canoes approaching the shore, were shouting furiously, and paddling with might and main to reach the spot, and stay their flight.

Half blinded, burnt and furious, Saunders saw that both he and his associates were lost if they hesitated; with a fearful malediction he shook his clenched hand at Arthur, who, scorched and choking, could not prevent his departure, jöined the men, who seized their canoe, carried it over the sand hill and launching it in the sea beyond, instantly paddled along the coast out of reach of their enraged enemies, the Woolwas, who did not attempt to follow them.

Arthur and Joe, scorched as they were, and a little bewildered by the nearly fatal contest they had been engaged in, breathed freely when they beheld the flight of Saunders and his comrades, and saw the patpans of the the Woolwas paddling swiftly ashore with comparative indifference.

Our hero knew not that the Woolwas were the furious enemies of the Mexicans, and their loud shouts, and war cries, and desperate gestures he thought might be directed against himself and Joe, as well as against the fugitives.

"Be gor! let us fly into the woods, sir," said Joe, gazing at the Indians in the canoes just touching the shore; "faix, they'll murder us."

"We should make a bad race of it, Joe, against Indians," replied our hero.

The Indians, as soon as their canoes reached

the shore, leaped out; several, with spears in their hands, rushed over the sand hills after Saunders and his comrades. To the fugitives' surprise, amongst some women who came ashore was the girl they had met in the hut. The women, and the young Indian girl, with three men came towards Arthur Bolton; the girl, by signs and smiles, giving him to understand that they were friends, and all exclaimed, "Englis, Englis!" as if pleased, but no other mode of communication existed. Joined by the other men, who soon returned from their fruitless pursuit after Saunders, all surrounded our hero, and examined him and Joe with great surprize. One old Indian, seeing they were scorched and burnt, went down to the canoes, and returned with a calabash, which he gave to the women.

Without any ceremony they insisted on pulling off their scorched clothes and then anointed them all over with the contents of the calabash. This gave them immense relief; but our hero, though he could not help a smile, felt exceedingly uncomfortable with the remarkable scanty clothing left him. The hut had been totally consumed, but the Indians drew up their canoes, and collecting branches and stakes, soon constructed two small huts, to hold their weapons, tools, &c., and to serve as shelter for their wives. The party had come to spend a few days, according to custom, turtle hunting. Fire was kindled out of the debris of the hut, and preparations made for cooking supper.

These Indians, our hero thought, were a very fine comely race, and the women exceeding good looking. "I will remain with the party till to-morrow," he said to himself, "and then get one of them to guide me to the river where the brig is stranded."

The Indian girl, whose name he discovered was Achupa, informed him, by signs, that the men were going to hunt turtles on some small Islands called Cays, three miles from the shore, and that they would not return to their village for eight days, holding up her fingers, she touched them one by one.

Arthur Bolton so improved on making signs, that he made Achupa understand that he wanted a little more clothing.

The girl laughed merrily, and going to her mother, a very fine looking woman, she spoke to her. The females all laughed; but Achupa's mother went to one of the canoes and took out of a plantain basket a long roll of red and blue striped cotton, and made signs to him to dress as they did, but our hero wonderfully objected to so primitive a custom, as it would expose him to the unmitigated attack of the mosquitoes, he preferred the remnants of his cotton trowsers, but necessity is ingenious; and with the assistance of Achupa, he manufactured what he considered a most excellent covering for his own and Joe's back and chest; with this addition to his attire they felt considerably better.

Their supper consisted of maize, plantains,

papayas, and stripes of manitas broiled, and some fish caught in the Lagoon.

The males of the party seemed very taciturn, spoke little and looked serious. The women were quite the contrary.

All this time our hero felt intense uneasiness; he could not banish from his mind the idea that Saunders would lead his desperate associates to plunder the brig. The situation of the females, therefore, in their unprotected situation was too horrible to think of.

Knowing how uncomfortable a journey would be without shoes, Bolton determined to adopt the Indian moccasins; and again his good genius, Achupa, provided them with a pair each. Joe passed part of the night in manufacturing two hats out of the broad-leaved flaggers, and they answered the purpose admirably. With energy and perseverance man can accomplish much, and with very inadequate means.

When everything was cleared away the

women retired to their huts. Some of the men to the canoes; two kept watch, whilst our hero and Joe passed the remainder of the night under two poles stretched across the canoes, with their light mat sails spread over them. Arthur did not expect or care to sleep, for he had much to occupy his thoughts. The oil applied to his burns had wonderfully relieved the pain, in fact he scarcely experienced any annoyance. Joe, having nothing particular to think of, and being free from pain, soon fell asleep. Towards morning our hero enjoyed two or three hours' repose, and only awoke hearing the voices of the women when they came to take some things out of the canoe.

CHAPTER II.

The party of Woolwa Indians that arrived so opportunely to the assistance of Arthur Bolton and Joe, belonged to a tribe, residing some distance from the sea shore, and were now on their annual visit to the Lagoons.

The Woolwas were particularly friendly with the settlers at Bluefields and traded with the English residents there.

They knew the difference between the English and Spaniards and Mexicans; they esteemed the first, but the latter they detested.

When our hero awoke in the morning he found that all the men and women, excepting Achupa and her mother, had carried their canoes across the sands, and were gone turtle hunting; they had removed their canoes without waking them by putting props under the poles.

Achupa's small canoe was the only one left. After making a hearty breakfast, prepared by the young Indian girl and her mother, Arthur, whose mind was bent upon reaching the Punza Pulca river, which he now felt satisfied communicated by some creek or stream with the Tonza Lagoon, commenced a conversation by signs with Achupa.

After a considerable amount of signs and drawing figures on the sand of Lagoons and rivers, he got the young girl to understand, that he wanted to go the Punza Pulca River.

When she thoroughly understood him, she pointed to her canoe, and then to the west, and with a stick, very clearly showed him on the sand, that he must cross the Lagoon and keep along shore to the setting sun; he would then see a broad creek running out of the Lagoon into the Punza Pulca river, but it was in places, a rapid dangerous stream, for it appeared that the Lagoon partly emptied itself into the river where the "Foam" lay.

The next thing was to get Achupa to lend him the canoe. She understood him at length, and that there were English in a ship in the Punza Pulca. She spoke a long time with her mother, and then they both made signs to him to take the canoe; the young girl, with a serious face, taking his hand, and by various most significant signs, making him promise to come back before eight days went by. This he sincerely promised to do, if alive.

Mother and daughter then put some provisions into a basket, together with a calabash of water, and assisted to carry the canoe to the water, where our hero and Joe joyfully embarked, after the most friendly leave taking from mother and daughter; indeed Achupa felt inclined to acompany them, and looked quite sorrowful when our hero waved his hand in adieu.

"Faix, sir," said Joe, flourishing one of the paddles in a very doubtful manner, and thereby nearly upsetting the light bark they were in. "Faix, sir, it is dangerous to sneeze in this here craft, she's as ticklish as my father's ould mare, be gorra; many's the toss the jade gave me, as I took the fruit to market."

"Then you were a bog trotter, Joe, before you became a sailor," returned our hero, plying his paddle cautiously.

"Be dad, you're right, sir; my father's cabin was in the middle of the great Bog of Allen, and many's the trot I and the ould mare have had over the soft turf."

"Do not put your paddle so far out, or so deep, Joe, with a little practice we shall get on; we were nearly becoming Indians, as far as attire went, and if we have much to do in such crafts as these, we shall be able to join a tribe with some degree of credit, if left in this country."

"Be gor, sir, it's not a bad country at all, barring the musquitoes; the girls are very comely, only their skin is a bit too red and brown."

Just then Joe missed his stroke with the paddle, and fell against our hero, nearly upsetting the canoe in the middle of the lake.

"Hallo, Joe! you must leave the red and brown girls alone, we should have a long swim, if our craft went over here."

"Faix, sir, I'm not thinking of the beauties at all; I hopes to get back to ould Ireland some of these days, and I should not like to take my ould father a red wife."

In a short time they came up with the opposite shore, on which grew some noble trees, forming a dense forest to the eastward as far as the eye could trace; they could by this time impel the canoe along with considerable swiftness and steadiness, keeping near shore, and continuing west and north, were they at length caught sight of a tolerable wide creek running to the north.

Into this creek they urged the canoe, and discovered as it grew narrower that there was a considerable current; after a short space the channel narrowed to twenty yards, and the stream increased in swiftness, running nearly six miles an hour, but so smooth and deep that their velocity was scarcely perceptible, except when regarding the shore on each side.

As our hero proceeded, his anxiety to reach the brig increased to a painful degree; a thousand distracting thoughts flitted through his brain; paramount amongst which was his anxiety whether Saunders had yet visited the brig, or whether he was projecting to do so.

As the canoe floated past the shores on each side of the inlet, the Englishmen were surprised at the wildness of the scenery; apparently no human foot had traversed the land, and yet the scenery was magnificent; the grass was of great height, great clumps of gum arabic bushes, knots of huge pine trees, with here and there a magnificent palm tree, grew luxuriantly. Beyond a great mango swamp, innumerable parrots chattered in the trees, scream-

-ing as they shot by them; whilst the cotton trees swarmed with them. Presently a sound like a fall of water fell upon their ears, and the canoe, only steered by a paddle, proceeded with great swiftness.

"It will be hard work, Joe, to return by this stream; but hark! we are approaching a fall or a rapid; sit steady, leave me to guide the craft."

The next instant the canoe shot down a rapid of considerable length, studded with huge rocks. Joe held his breath, and grasped both sides, for the rapid was an exceedingly dangerous one, but Arthur Bolton was cool and collected, and watching the rocks, he steered quite clear of the dangers and even escaped the whirlpool at the bottom by a few strokes of the paddle, and they were in still water, with scarcely a perceptible run, but a moment's examination shewed our hero that the tide reached to the foot of the fall, and that along the shore on the eastern side there was a kind of towing path leading along the fall.

"Faix, I thought it was all over with us, sir," said Joe, regaining his breath. "We can never ascend that rapid."

"No," replied Arthur Bolton. "I see now that the Indians carry their canoes past the fall. Yonder is a kind of path trampled through the thickets. I am satisfied we are all right; the tide proves we shall run shortly into the Punza Pulca."

After two hours' paddling they emerged from the creek into the great stream of the Punza Pulca, the creek having a great mango swamp on each side.

Arthur Bolton gazed anxiously down the stream, but a projecting and thickly-wooded point from the opposite shore shut out the broad estuary where the "Foam" lay stranded.

Paddling across, they had just reached the point when they were hailed by a voice from the shore. Ceasing paddling, our voyagers turned their attention to where the sound came from, and beheld a negro pushing through the bushes and getting out on a projecting rock, hailed again.

"That's a black man," said Arthur Bolton, "in European clothing, let us go to him."

Urging the canoe close into the rock, they looked at the black, particularly before they let the canoe touch the rock. We need not describe him, for it was Cato the black cook of the "Maria Gloriosa."

The black stared at them with much greater surprise.

"Holly, . golly! What! you be no Indians."

".No," said Arthur Bolton, "we are English. Where do you come from?"

"Me cook to the Guarda Costa, Massa; me come from de brig. Pray, where you come from?"

Arthur started, and pushing to the rock, he exclaimed,

"You come from the brig? Are all the females well aboard?"

"Golly, massa! dey be gone to Bluefields, but the young missy de dam Sambos and de Mexican thiefs ab carried away."

A terrible feeling came over Arthur; terror took possession of his mind and paralyzed him. The black looked at him; he saw the start and the change of countenance, and though puzzled, he said, "Me now go look for missey; but me can no cross de riber. You take me in canoe. Me sure find missy."

In a few minutes, Arthur Bolton recovering the shock, pushed ashore and heard all the particulars as well as Cato could explain them. His beautiful Alice was in the power of the Sambos, for she certainly was not with Saunders and his associates, and his mind was made up at once.

"Now, jump out, Joe. I will land this noble-hearted fellow on the other side of the creek; he will follow in the track of the Sambos. I will come back for you, for the canoe will not hold three. We will proceed to the brig, resume our clothes, and well-armed, follow Cato. No time must be lost. Jump out."

Joe wished the canoe would hold three; he did not much like the look of the place where he was to wait his master's return, but Cato consoled him by stating, "No wild beast eat you up till dark; you quite safe for dat."

"Be gor, they shan't eat me by day or night," thought Joe.

And the moment the canoe pushed off and was out of sight he climbed up a tree and ensconced himself in the branches. But Joe was by no means aware, that a very large monkey was seated above, eagerly watching his movements, and, as he did not look up, he suddenly received a sharp stroke from the beast's paw, the beast uttering a frightful scream at the same time, and jumping on a higher branch.

Joe was paralysed, the perspiration literally poured from his forehead. He thought his hour was come, and in an agony of fright—though as brave a boy in affairs of actual life as could be—he roared, and implored the help of every saint in the Irish calendar. But the monkey beat him hollow in his ejaculations, screaming and chattering, and making hideous faces.

Joe, half dead with fright, at last looked up, and there beheld his enemy swinging by the tail to a branch, and uttering all kinds of cries, and twisting himself into every kind of shape; and then, becoming quiet, shewed his teeth, and spat like a cat at his enemy.

"Oh!" said Joe, wiping the moisture from his forehead and eyes, "it's you, is it. Be gor, I thought 'twas a bear. Faix, I'll pay you off for this; the Lord save us! I'm just as if I was hoisted out of the river."

He then got astride on a branch, and surveyed his enemy.

"A monkey! faix, he's a big, ugly customer; but, be dad, I'll have him out of that."

And he commenced breaking off a stout

branch; but as he did so, he heard a great crash of branches below, and looking down, to his inconceivable terror, beheld a huge beast breaking through the brushwood, and coming towards the river.

It was what the natives call a tapir, not unlike a wild boar, but very much larger, the back highly arched, with a kind of proboscis hanging over the mouth, and which the animal uses in the manner of the elephant. The skin is so hard that it will resist a musket ball. Now, though the beast is so formidable to look at, it is perfectly harmless, and lives on plants and roots, and can exist in the water for a time.

As the beast came towards the tree on which sat the stupified Joe, the immense ape above him, which afterwards turned out to be a tame one, escaped from a native village, gave a scream, and sprang on Joe's shoulders. Joe roared with fright, lost his hold, and fell, actually pitching on the back of the tapir, which luckily broke his fall. The astonishment of the beast was equal to Joe's terror; it bellowed with fear, and, crashing through the trees, plunged into the stream, and swam out of sight.

"The Lord be merciful to us, he's gone," muttered Joe, venturing to rise; "it's a mercy that every bone in my carcass wasn't broke. Bad cess to the beast, its backbone was like a rod of iron."

And carefully examining his limbs, and stretching out his arms, he looked round for the ape, but he too had disappeared. He then scrambled out on the rock, and to his infinite joy beheld Arthur Bolton returning.

"The saints be glorified!" ejaculated Joe. "I ain't a coward, neither; but, faix, with a monkey as big as a man above you, and an elephant below, be gor it requires a stout heart not to be frightened. I was not afeard of the ape, be dad, I'd have settled him in no time; only the brute was so infernally nimble, and hung so by his tail. Faix, swinging by a tail ain't a bad thing at times, but inconvenient with one's clothes on."

Arthur paddled to the rock, exclaiming—

"Jump in, Joe, we have no time to lose. The sun will be down in an hour."

"Faix, Mr. Bolton, it's myself has had a great escape entirely," said Joe, getting into the canoe. "Sure, I was near drowned, sir, by an elephant and an ape."

"An elephant!" said Arthur Bolton, laughing, "why, you're dreaming, Joe: there are neither apes nor elephants in this part of the world."

"Oh, be dad, then, they are out of their reckoning, and were cast ashore like ourselves, for I see'd or felt them both." And Joe described his adventure with the beasts.

Arthur laughed heartily.

"Your story surprises me, but elephant it could not be, though it had what you call a trunk; there are, I know, some strange animals in these forests; but elephants there are none, and from your description the animal was more like a wild pig."

"Be dad," returned Joe, laughing, "he was a big pig, and had a mighty fine snout of his own for picking up the praties."

Just then they turned the point, and beheld the brig.

"What did you do with the negro, sir?" asked Joe.

"I put him ashore on the far side of the creek. He is well armed, and has money, and says he will be sure to find out where those wretches have carried Miss Alice Marchmont. I promised to follow as soon as we had obtained clothing and arms. He strongly advised our return to the Woolwas, and to accompany them to their village. I should most likely find him there, and the Woolwas were sure to help us against the Sambos, in rescuing the young lady."

Paddling along as fast as they could, they soon reached the side of the brig. The Spaniards on board looked at them with great surprise. But Arthur, ascending the side, soon made the officer left in charge of the vessel understand him.

Mrs. Marchmont, before her departure, had told Capt. Castinos all about our hero and his companion, Joe, in case they should return, and requested him to state the same to his mate, whom he had left on board; therefore our hero experienced no difficulty in proving to the mate who he was, and in making him understand what he intended doing to rescue Miss Alice.

"You must be very cautious," said the mate. "Courajo, those Mexican dogs are real cut-throats, they have committed I don't know how many murders. They stole a schooner from Nicaragua, and killed the padrone and one man and a boy. As to the Sambos, they are a drunken, besotted race, capable of anything brutal and ferocious when indulging in what they call a 'big drunk.' Without Cato you will have no chance; his advice to stay with the Woolwas was good."

Early the next morning, our hero resumed his usual attire, and concealing a considerable sum in dollars and gold in a belt fastened round the waist, he and Joe prepared to depart with the first of the flood. For arms Arthur had an excellent double-barrelled fowling-piece, and Joe a rifle, and a brace of pistols each. A basket of provisions, and some flasks of rum, and a jar of brandy for the Woolwas, was also put in the canoe. Taking leave of Juan Peraz, the mate, a remarkably kind, civil Spaniard, our hero and Joe entered the canoe, and pushed off from the brig.

As it was possible the brig might be taken to Bluefields before their return, the mate advised them to take Cato for a guide, and to cross the country to that place, as by so doing they would be sure to come across the party that Mrs. Marchmont would despatch from Bluefields.

Paddling up the river with the tide, our hero remarked to Joe that the weather, though then calm, looked anything but pleasant. The mate had also remarked it, and said that heavy thunder storms and tremendous rains were very frequent at that period of the year.

"We shall barely reach the creek before we have a storm, Joe," said Arthur.

Joe looked up, and saw that dense masses of clouds were advancing from the south, and that a brisk breeze was rising. He remembered his adventures the day before, and by no means relishing the idea of passing the night in the woods, he redoubled his exertions. An immense flock of the blue-winged teal passing within thirty yards, induced Arthur Bolton to load with shot, and try to bag a few. Fifteen teal he shot with both barrels, besides many wounded, which he would not pursue, for the breeze was increasing, and the sky threatening. Just as they gained the creek, and got within its waters, the storm burst, with thunder and lightning, and furious gusts of wind, but no rain. He urged on the canoe, so as to gain the foot of the falls, for when descending the rapid our hero observed that a lofty range of rock, pierced with several openings like caverns, stood exposed on the further shore. As the rain was sure to come down in torrents, Arthur was extremely anxious to reach this shelter before it began, for he saw it was quite impossible to carry the canoe past the rapid that day, as the rain and storm would no doubt last for hours. It was with exceeding difficulty they kept the canoe afloat. The gusts of wind threatened to force her out of the water, and the roar of the blast, as it swept through the trees, crushing and breaking the branches, and hurling them over the creek, almost equalled the thunder in uproar. Keeping close in under the bank, the storm swept over them, and just as some immense drops of rain began to fall, they reached the foot of the rapid, almost breathless from their exertions.

"Now be quick, Joe," said our hero, jumping ashore, "There are the rocks, lay hold of the canoe, in five minutes we shall have a deluge."

Seizing the light canoe, they easily bore her to the rocks, and as the rain began to descend in a marvellous torrent, they gained shelter in a large and spacious cavern.

"Come, this is indeed fortunate," said our hero, as they placed the canoe on a gravelly bottom, and then turned to look at a tropical downpour of rain. The thunder rolled to a distance, the lightning, considering it was yet daylight, was brilliant and incessant; but soon ceased, for the storm passed on with great rapidity; the deluge of rain, however, ran by the mouth of the cave like a deep river, and this continued till nearly dusk, when the clouds broke.

"We are here for the night," said Arthur, "so let us make ourselves as comfortable as we can. Take out the basket, Joe, and we will sup—why it's a perfect river running by the mouth of the cave. This stream from the summit of these rocks will make the fall very rapid to-morrow."

"Faix, sir, I hope none of those beasts I saw yesterday will take it into their head to come and sleep here."

"Not much fear of that, Joe, with such a stream running by our door. I wish we had some wood, we could make a fire and smother out these abominable mosquitoes, far worse enemies than the hog that frightened you."

"Be dad!' muttered Joe, "I never seed a hog with a probosus a yard long over his snout."

Having satisfied their appetites, they next sought out a dry spot on which to pass the night, and a long dismal one it was; but our voyagers, nevertheless, contrived to get a few hours' rest, though Joe felt exceedingly disinclined to sleep, for various strange sounds and hisses were distinctly heard coming from the forest and jungle round the cavern.

The morning broke fine and beautiful with a refreshing breeze, and the air cooled by the storm of the past night. The stream before the cavern had become a rill, and the parrots and parroquets were chattering and screaming with might and main.

Having breakfasted on the contents of the basket, they then rubbed and brushed up the guns and pistols, and loaded them with ball, excepting one barrel of the fowling piece, which was kept loaded with shot for any kind of game that might come in their way.

They had to carry the canoe a full mile before launching her, but Arthur had adopted an easy manner of carrying her, by suspending her on a light pliant pole, each supporting an end. It was very evident that the Indians who navigated this creek always carried their canoes past the rapid, when going to the Lagoon of La Tonza, for a narrow path bordering the stream was visible, the thick brushwood being cut away and the branches cleared. Still it was a rough and tiresome path. They had nearly accomplished their task when the loud and peculiar whoop of Indians struck upon their ears.

They paused, and looking in the direction of the sound, to their surprise beheld a large canoe and a patpan just shooting the fall. The canoe was full of Indians, the patpan, a broad, shallow flat boat, held Saunders and the Mexican desperadoes. Though they flitted by like a flash of lightning, Saunders had recognized them, and with a yell of exultation fired his musket at them, but without effect.

"Now then, Joe, our lives are at stake; there's not a moment to be lost; they will pursue us on foot the moment they reach the level."

Exerting themselves to the utmost, they reached the level and launched the canoe, and then commenced urging her up the stream towards the Lagoon. Loud shouts shortly after were heard in the woods, proving that they were pursued. Arthur had loaded his second barrel with ball, determined to make a desperate resistance, and if possible put an end to the career of that villain, Saunders. If their pursuers were on foot and did not carry their canoes with them, they had every chance of escaping, as they could land on the opposite shore and shelter themselves behind the immense trees on its banks.

CHAPTER III.

It was a very critical trial for our voyagers, for their enemies were numerous and vindictive, and their shouts and menaces, and howls of rage resounded through the woods. Presently they came into view, ten of them carrying the long Indian canoe.

"Now be steady and cool, Joe," said our hero to his young assistant; "those Mexican scoundrels have fire arms."

A shout of exultation broke from the Mexicans, and a yell of savage delight from the Sambos when they beheld those they hunted.

They were still musket shot distant, but with six paddles in their canoe they would soon gain on them. Joe was but weak, and could not handle his paddle as well as Arthur Bolton.

They could see two of the Mexicans standing up in the canoe with muskets in their hands, watching, no doubt, till near enough to fire. On flew the light canoe, but Joe's power was not equal to the powerful strokes of Arthur Bolton's paddle, so consequently he had to keep the craft straight and to use only half his power.

The Indian canoe came rapidly up with them, and so eager was Saunders for the blood of his intended victim that he fired the moment they were within a hundred yards; the ball went through the side of the canoe, making poor Joe's heart beat faster. Luckily the hole was two inches above water.

Bolton's blood boiled; checking his paddle, he seized his gun. They were not more than eighty yards from the Indians. Another shot, the ball whizzing close to Arthur's cheek. He could distinguish Saunders and one of the Mexicans standing erect, whilst the Sambos urged on the canoe. Saunders was reloading, when, taking a steady aim at the wretch, he fired. With a yell of rage Saunders staggered, and fell on the side of the canoe, which instantly upset, sending her entire crew into the creek. Joe gave a cheer of genuine delight, and then both seized their paddles and urged the canoe towards the Lagoon.

"Faix, sir," said Joe; "the rascal's got it this time. Thanks to the saints, it was right in his locker."

A bend in the creek shut those struggling in the water from their sight. Ten minutes more and the canoe shot into the lake.

"Thank God!" said our hero, "that was a fortunate shot. The villain's fall overturned the canoe; no doubt they can all swim, but I think before they can right their canoe and get ashore, and re-embark, we shall be too far for pursuit. Just put a plug in that hole, for the Lagoon is rough, and the breeze is against us."

The wind blew so fresh that they were forced to keep along shore, and for two hours made little or no progress, till turning a point of land, they got some shelter. To cross the lake till the breeze decreased was impossible; so lifting the canoe upon the beach, they resolved to wait till the sun set, when the breeze, as it was from the sea, would most probably cease.

As Arthur conjectured, the sea breeze slackened considerably, as the sun declined; so launching their canoe, they paddled across the Lagoon. Every hour's delay appeared to Arthur an age; he was perpetually thinking of his beautiful Alice, exposed to all the horrors of a captivity amongst the brutal Sambos, and was selfish enough to rejoice that she had the companionship of her devoted attendant Mary Pearson; and he hoped, too, that the Sambos only detained her to extort ransom. He was also buoyed up with the idea that he had killed Saunders; at all events, wounded him, which would for a time prevent him from committing further atrocities.

It was quite dusk before they reached the spot where they had left the Indians; but their approach was perceived, for our hero observed some women holding pine torches, on the beach. As soon as the canoe touched the shore, and he leaped out, he was surrounded by the women, and welcomed with smiles by Achupa, who, waving her torch, gazed at our hero, considerably surprised by his and Joe's change of garment. Several of the men looked delighted at the fire-arms, and one tall fellow, taking up the jar full of rum put it to his nose, and then with a strange gesticulation, cut several singular antics, to show that the contents of the jar pleased him greatly. Still none of them touched the fire-arms, or attempted to appropriate anything in the canoe, only carried them up to the huts, of which there were now several; Achupa making signs to Arthur, that their party was increased by eight or ten men. She also strove to make our hero understand that the new comers were great chiefs, and very friendly. As they reached the front of the huts, there came forth an Indian in a costume, that somewhat astounded our hero, and so amused Joe, that he could scarcely keep his countenance. He was a tall stately man, in the prime of life. He wore a very short check shirt, and an old naval uniform coat, with long tails, and a lieutenant's cocked hat; other garments he had none, if we except a pair of sandals or mocassins. The rest of the Indians assembled around him, showing him great respect. The Indian raised his cocked hat, and advancing, held out his hand, saying, in English: "How do you do, sar? Very glad to see you, sar. Me chief of de Woolwas; and me name—Punka Bosswash Cookra Malagalpa Rama."

"Be St. Peter," muttered Joe, in a low voice, "there's a stinger of a name,—Punka Pigswash!—Holy Moses!" As the Chief shook our hero cordially by the hand, he looked sharply at Joe, whose muttered sentence had evidently reached his ears. Arthur Bolton rejoiced to hear English spoken, and thanked the Chief, saying he was most happy in making his acquaintance, and begged his acceptance of a jar of rum.

"Holly golly, Sir! me very glad, drink your health," and taking the jar, he removed the cork and took a steady pull.

"Faix, that's no Pigswash, anyhow," muttered Joe, as the Indian drew a long breath.

"De rum very good, and—"and making a sign, one of the Indians brought the half of a cocoa nut shell, and all surrounded their Chief, who gave each about a wine glass full, and then corking the jar, handed it to one of his wives to take care of.

Punka Bosswash, as we shall call him, then ordered our hero's effects to be carried to one of the huts which he intended for his sole use, and then said he would change his dress and visit him by and by. All hands began preparing a meal which served for their supper. Achupa seemed quite pleased and most anxious to be of use. She lighted a fire before their hut, and assisted Joe, who felt quite at home with the Indian girl, in toasting a couple of blue teal for supper. She brought them plenty of yams, and water in a gourd, and when all was ready, with a smile, left them to themselves.

"Gosh, Sir, Mr. Pigswash knows how to suck the monkey first rate."

"Punka Bosswash is the name, Joe," said Arthur Bolton, with a smile. "Indians are excessively sensitive of ridicule. This Indian Chief speaks English tolerably well, and no doubt has passed many years of his life in Jamaica, or where English is spoken. I have now great hopes of being able to induce this Chief to assist me in the search after Miss Alice Marchmont—and no time must be lost."

"I wonder, Sir, has the Black Cato come upon the track of the villains that carried her off. Faix, sir, I hope you have killed the desperate villain, Saunders, anyhow."

"I shall certainly not regret having done so."

Whilst conversing, and Joe having cleared away the remnants of their supper, Punka Bosswash entered the hut and sat down upon a log of wood. He had laid aside his costume of coat and cocked hat, and appeared like the rest of his tribe, saving that he wore a species of coronet round his head, in which was placed two very handsome feathers of some native bird.

"Me come have big talk wid you, Sar," said the Chief, filling his pipe with tobacco and then lighting it. "My daughter, Achupa, say you English, and me lub de English much—and me tell you how I came speak English, and den you tell, where you come from, and what you do in this country, widout ship or much company."

Arthur Bolton had a small jar of brandy and forthwith helped the chief to a glass, which he relished exceedingly, and having puffed at his pipe for a few moments, he gave our hero the following account of himself:

His father, he said, was a great Chief, but when he was nine years old the Sambos made an attack on their village with a party of Mexican villains and plundered it, and carried him and some other boys and girls off from the squaws—for the men of the village were all out at a great hunting party. The Sambos took him and others to a place on the coast and sold them to an American trader. They were afterwards wrecked on the Island of Jamaica; but though the ship was lost, the crew and all on board were saved. The American Captain sold him to an English Planter, whose name he thought was Copeland. He was very ill-used for four or five years; but after that, he fell into the hands of better masters, and finally, when grown up, and married, was sold, together with his little one to a rich English Merchant, named Marchmont. On the mention of this name, our hero started and became much more interested.

The tale proved, as it proceeded, that Mr. Marchmont and his good wife were the best people in the world, and when the emancipation of the negroes took place, they restored him and his wife and family to their own country laden with presents. When he rejoined his countrymen he was elected chief, his father having just died. He had recently visited Jamaica, and was just returned; he had seen his good master, Mr. Marchmont, who was expecting his wife and daughters from England. And now, sar," continued the Woolwa chief, having finished his story, and two cocoa nuts full of brandy, "what you here for? and what me can do for you, for I lub de whites, and de English much more—"

Arthur at once made Punka Bosswash acquainted with the state of affairs. He told him of the wreck of the Foam, and of Miss Marchmont being in the hands of the Sambos and the Mexican desperadoes, headed by the villain who had murdered Captain Courtney. The astonishment of Punka Bosswash was great indeed; he became quite excited, muttered all kinds of Indian expressions, and finally told our hero, that he would break up the turtle expedition, and return at once to their settlement. He would then call a council, and, with a party, attack the Sambos of Quamwatta, where he felt sure Miss Alice Marchmont was held captive.

This determination of the chief greatly pleased our hero, and when Punka Bosswash departed, he shook him most cordially by the hand.

The next morning all the turtle party were busy packing up. Achupa came, and by signs and words told our hero that he and Joe should keep her canoe for themselves; they would like it better than being in the larger canoes, with her countrymen.

This arrangement suited our hero's wishes, and he thanked the chief's daughter for all her kindness.

Having finished their morning meal, the canoes were launched, and, all being ready, the whole party pushed out into the lagoon. Arthur and Joe in their light craft, kept up easily with the larger canoes. Passing across the lagoon, the little fleet kept away to the eastward, the chief's canoe leading. Arthur, now that he was positively on the track of his beloved Alice, became more calm and collected. He would sacrifice life or release her, and he confidently hoped, that though she must be in a fearful situation, she was free from the horrors of being in the power of Saunders. The Sambos, greedy of gain, no doubt joined in carrying her off for the sake of ransom, whilst Saunders' efforts were directed to the plunder of the brig.

The lagoon of La Tonza formed one of those singular lakes that, joining each other by narrow creeks and channels, continue along the Mosquito coast, as far as Cape Gracias, forming an immense inland navigation, bordering the sea coast, at times merely separated by a belt of sand. These lakes extend a distance of one hundred and sixty miles.

Having crossed the lagoon, they turned a bold point to the eastward, and entered a wide creek, which brought them to a long, narrow piece of water; paddling its entire length, they entered a narrow, and somewhat rapid channel, which ran in a westerly direction, and drawing up alongside an island, their fires were lighted, and their food prepared and eaten. Punka Bosswash informed our hero that they would reach their village the next day; that they would camp where they were, as they had to ascend a rapid river, which required daylight to accomplish.

On the spot where the Indians had cooked their meals vegetation flourished in the greatest luxuriance. Here, for the first time, Arthur beheld the graceful and gigantic ceiba, or silk cotton tree; it was then in bloom; on the summit of this beautiful tree was a crown of flowers, in rich profusion of various colours, but chiefly bright carnation.

It was nearly eighty feet high, and almost five feet in diameter. The perfume was almost overpowering, whilst the ground beneath was covered with its gay blossoms.

The natives take the cotton from the pods, which succeed the flowers; when ripe, they burst open, the inside being full of a silky fibre, of soft, light cotton. The Woolwa chief told Arthur Bolton that the chief use they made of the tree was for making canoes and dories, as it rarely splits from the heat of the sun, and is besides, light and buoyant.

The next morning they started very early, and, after shooting two rapids, entered a broad, noble river, which our hero thought was the Punza Pulca river; but he learned afterwards that it was the Rio Grande, that led by a creek into the Bosswash river.

The scenery, on entering the latter river, was diversified and beautiful. Two hours before sunset they came in sight of the great village of the Woolwa chief—a long range of huts on the right bank of the river. Around the village were extensive plantations of Cassava, and all kinds of fruit and vegetables were visible in abundance.

The appearance of the turtle fleet returning from their hunting expedition, brought out all the inhabitants, old and young, of the village. Our hero and his attendant were regarded with considerable surprise and curiosity. Their chief, in his quiet way, made them all acquainted as to who his guests were, and at once they ceased to be troublesome by crowding round them, eyeing their guns with eager scrutiny.

Achupa and her mother conducted them to a commodious hut, which was to be their exclusive abode, and an Indian girl and Achupa attended to their wants, providing them with food, fire, &c.

"Well, be dad, sir," said Joe, depositing the guns and pistols, after carefully wiping them, in a corner of the hut, which consisted of only one room, "they are a quiet, kind, comely people, and one soon gets accustomed to the rather scanty clothing they wear."

"Yes, Joe, they are kind and hospitable; very different from the Sambo race. I shudder when I think of poor Miss Alice Marchmont, amongst such a most uncivilised, drunken, vicious race. I trust Punka Bosswash will not delay our expedition beyond to-morrow. Perhaps Cato may arrive either to-night or to-morrow, he could reach her by a shorter way than we came."

"May be, sir, he is spying out where the villains keep the young lady and her attendant—that may delay him."

"Most likely, Joe—just keep up the smoke by putting on some damp wood—those confounded mosquitoes are bent upon mischief."

"Faix, sir, it's a hard case; we must either consent to be suffocated or murdered entirely by those beasts, bad cess to them. Be dad, if we were dressed after the fashion of Mr.

Bogwash, they'd eat us entirely—our skins are more tender, I suppose?"

Having finished their supper and smoked out the mosquitoes, they retired to rest on the bundles of dried, scented leaves of some peculiar plants selected for that purpose, and with which Achupa and her attendant had well supplied the hut.

CHAPTER IV.

When Alice, with her devoted attendant Mary, was seized and carried off, her despair almost deprived her of existence. Mary, with tender affection and that total carelessness of self, which distinguished her, supported her throbbing temples upon her breast, and, in whispered words, strove to encourage hope in her heart when, alas! hope was almost dead within her own breast.

Saunders gazed upon his victims, as the Indians paddled up the river, with fiendish exultation:—

"So," said he, fixing his savage eye upon Mary, "you all thought you had done with

William Saunders; but my turn is now come. I will have a terrible revenge on you all—an eye for an eye—I will gouge out that accursed Bolton's eye, as he did mine, and then put him to a death of torture!"

"Miserable wretch, whose hands are dyed with innocent blood, do you think there is no God hearing and watching you?" said Alice, raising her head and letting her eyes, for a moment, rest, with indignation, upon the hideous face of the miserable Saunders. "God will protect us still, and your own fate will yet be even more terrible than that your brutal imagination pictures for your victim."

Mary Pearson trembled all over; she feared her young mistress's words would rouse the furious passions of the wretch in whose power they were.

Saunders gazed, bewildered, for a moment at the excited maiden, whose steady gaze never quailed before the ruffian's glare. The spirit of the young girl, never before roused or tried, was visible in her beautiful features and dark, flashing eyes. Alice, from that moment, cast aside the timidity of her nature, and resolved to face her destiny with a firm reliance upon Providence.

"Well, curse me," muttered Saunders, "if you an't a young vixen and no mistake; blow me, but I think after all that you'll make an excellent wife for a bold adventurer, and mine you shall be at all events;" and with a horrid laugh he added—"and your pretty attendant there, will do for the second. My jolly friends, the Sambos, allow a man two wives, so thank your stars you will not be separated."

Alice, with a look of scorn and defiance, turned away, and though her heart was throbbing with painful excitement, she made no reply.

The three boats proceeded rapidly up the river. Saunders and the Mexican desperado coolly conversing, in half Spanish and broken English, of their plans, being fully resolved to plunder and destroy the brig. In forty-eight hours they fully expected to get sufficient help to overpower those left in the vessel by the "Guarda Costa."

Crossing the stream, the canoes stopped at the mouth of the creek or channel leading into the Tonza Lagoon, and there a consultation took place between one of the Mexicans and the Sambos. Saunders and the Mexicans got into a canoe with the Sambos, whilst several Sambos took their place in the canoe with Alice Marchmont and her attendant.

"I leave you in good hands," said Saunders, as he left the boat; "don't fret after me. I'll be back with you in a day or two, and if I'm lucky I'll bring your fancy man, Bolton, back to witness our wedding," and with a horrid laugh, he left them, and with his comrades paddled up the channel leading to the Tonza Lagoon.

"Thank God," exclaimed Alice, clasping her hands, "that wretch and his comrades are gone. Hideous as these Sambos are, I feel a wonderful relief, even as their prisoner."

"Ah, Miss Alice," said Mary, "there is a chance of escape, depend on it, Mr. Bolton will get back to the brig, and when he hears of your being carried off, no power or persuasion will prevent him from pursuing our villanous enemies."

Whilst Alice and Mary Pearson were conversing, the Sambos in their canoe paddled up the stream for four or five miles, and crossing to the west side, went up another river or channel, and after an hour's paddling, entered a noble stream, down which they went at a rapid pace, preceded by the other canoe.

From this river they entered a lagoon just as the shades of night were covering the waters. They ran the canoes upon the beach before a large village of huts, with numerous dories, and patpans, and canoes hauled up before them.

A number of frightful looking Sambos, men, women, and children, crowded to the water's edge. Many of the men were drunk, and some of the women not much better.

The two unfortunate captives were horrified at the crowd; some of the women carried lighted pieces of pine wood, steeped in a kind of gum, which they flared about in a wild and reckless manner. One of the Sambos in the canoe seemed to have authority over the rest, for he spoke fiercely to the crowd, and made them fall back. To the surprise of the captives he turned to them, and spoke in broken English. He told them they should not be hurt, and should have a hut to themselves, and food, and a woman to attend on them, but if they attempted to escape they would be chained.

They were then helped ashore, and three or four women took charge of them, and talking and gesticulating, led them up the beach, followed by a lot of screaming children, of both sexes, without a particle of clothing, till they came to a hut, at some distance from the other huts, and into this miserable substitute for a dwelling they were forced to go.

The hut was tolerably large, neatly wattled

at the sides, and the door made of canes. Rough blocks of wood served in the place of seats, and a curious kind of frame, about a foot from the floor, and on which was a heap of soft leaves and fine hay, served as a bed. The two women, after sticking a kind of torch in the floor, retired, but shortly returned with two baskets, one containing cakes of corn meal, and some kind of broiled meat, and a calabash full of sweet wine, made from the palm, and not unpleasant to the taste. As the women placed those things before them, the Sambo who spoke English entered the hut, and, to the infinite disgust of Alice Marchmont, sat down on one of the logs of wood.

"Dat very good to eat," he said, pointing to the contents of the baskets, "no be afraid. To-morrow you will have cassava, squashes, and cocoa nut, and plantains."

"If," said Alice, forcing herself to look at the very hideous Sambo before her, his head all frizzled, and his face disfigured by a disgusting disease—a kind of leprosy, "if you have taken me from my protectors for the sake of gaining a large sum of money, I faithfully promise you, if you restore me to liberty, and conduct me either to Bluefields, or put me and my attendant on board the brig, you shall be paid, without question, a thousand dollars."

The Sambo started, repeating—

"A thousand dollars! dat big money! who pay dat?"

"My father will pay it cheerfully," said Alice; "and thank you for releasing me from that villain, Saunders, for he alone committed this outrage. You would not have done it—but for him."

"Him debble, no doubt, missy," said the Sambo, shaking his head. "He burn our huts, and kill us, if we let you go."

"Are you such cowards," said Alice, earnestly, "as to let five men terrify you?"

"Ja, missy; de be twenty men, with gun and pistol. De murder de women. De give me drink, and all go mad together."

"But, surely," said Alice, still hoping, "there are English in Bluefields?"

"Ja, Ja; no, missy; no Englis. De white people die in dis climate. No go, missy. De man English, and de oders say de hab you and de oda missy for wife, and de Sambo do nothing." And giving a ghastly smile, the Sambo chief left the hut.

"What a frightful wretch," said Mary, with a shudder. "Oh, if we could escape!"

"But where, Mary, could we go? We should die in the forests and swamps, or be killed by wild beasts. We do not know the country, and how cross the numerous rivers and lagoons. We must depend on Mr. Bolton; and no doubt my beloved mother will send persons in pursuit. The men in the cutter may be on our track. I do not fear the Sambos, though, by all accounts, they are a brutal, drunken race; but they would do anything for drink or money. It is that Saunders, and his vile associates, that I fear."

The night passed without any disturbance,

except the howling of dogs, of which great numbers were kept in the village. There was no window of any kind in the hut, but a large hole in the cane door, which did not open on the village, but towards the lagoon.

The women attended to their wants, and thus two miserable days past. Hot as it was, they were obliged to keep their doors shut, for sundry attacks to get in were made by legions of pigs, whose grunts and screams, as a score of half-starved dogs attacked them, distracted the ear. At night—to keep the mosquitoes out, they were forced to smother themselves till they were half suffocated. Still they kept up their spirits by hoping. What a blessing hope is!

On the third day, by the noise and confusion, pigs grunting, and dogs growling, and men shouting, and women screaming, our captives conjectured, and felt no little terror in doing so, that some kind of jollification was going on. About mid-day, the Sambo chief came into the hut, kicking and thumping three great hogs that wanted to rush in. Alice Marchmont's face flushed, for the brute was drunk, and had to support himself by leaning against the side of the hut.

"Well, missy," said the man, grinning, "how you do dis morning. Grand feast for six days. Your English husband come dis night, he berry glad see you; we have jollification for six days."

Alice gazed at Mary with a look of horror. "Good God! does this miserable wretch mean that the villain, Saunders, is coming?"

"Oh, Ja," interrupted the Sambo, maliciously, "dat is he; de all come; you hear fire gun—and de debbles big drunk." And with a horrible laugh, the Sambo reeled out of the hut, leaving the captives in a terrible state of anxiety.

"I will listen to your plan for escape now, Mary; even death in the woods would be better than to remain here, to become the victims of that vile wretch, Saunders, and his associates. Who can say what atrocities they may commit, when giving way to drink, and with such horrible wretches as these Sambos."

Mary Pearson was terrified—

"Yes, my beloved mistress, death would be preferable; they will be all drunk in this accursed village before dusk. Let us get into the woods, and trust to God's providence."

The unfortunate maidens made up their minds to trust to the chances of escape through the woods, and get, if possible, to the sea shore.

All day, the shouting, yelling, and frightful uproar continued, accompanied by the firing of guns—becoming more fast and furious as the sun set.

As soon as it was dark, Alice and Mary, with heavy hearts, opened the door of the hut, and gazed forth. The noise and uproar was behind them—for the hut they occupied was some little distance from the cluster. The lagoon lay before them, some two hundred yards off, but to the right of the hut, and quite close, was a thick belt of trees. None of the Sambos men or women watched the hut, for the prospect of a big drunk, in which the women always participated, drew the two females, who generally kept watch, away, to join the revellers.

With no other protection to their persons, than the shawls they had on when carried away from the brig, the fugitives crept cautiously from the hut. As Alice gazed into the dark forest and listened to the hideous noises, even then beginning, especially the howling monkey, she and Mary hesitated. Looking back at the village, they beheld huge fires, and the dark forms of the drinking Sambos men and women dancing furiously, for the strong glare of the fires revealed the figures and actions distinctly, as they gazed. They clearly beheld amongst them the figures of several Europeans, with guns, firing them off, and exciting the Sambo women into frantic dances. Suddenly Alice grasped Mary's arm, saying—

"Ah, there is that wretch Saunders—he is a head taller than the others."

"We can hesitate no longer," said Mary; "death will be better than the touch of that monster and murderer."

And then rapidily gliding across the space between the huts and the wood, they entered beneath the deep sombre shade of the latter. Whether some of the Sambos caught a glimpse of the fugitives, as they crossed the space, or Saunders himself happened to be casting a glance towards the hut, we cannot say, but scarcely had they entered beneath the trees before Saunders uttered a shout of alarm that the English girls had gone out of the hut, and were escaping into the forest.

Saunders, and two of his comrades, and three or four drunken Sambos, with torches, started in pursuit. Not ten yards from the spot where the maidens entered the wood, stretched upon the ground, hidden by the shrubs, and watching intently the proceedings of the revellers, was a tall and powerful negro. This watcher was Cato, the black cook of the Guarda Costa.

Starting up, he rushed after the fugitives, calling upon the maidens to stop, saying :—

"I am Cato! a good friend!"

Astounded, they hesitated, for they, of course, knew not who Cato was. Nevertheless, they paused, and the black stood beside them. In a few words he stated who he was, begged them to go back to the hut, and, as he now knew where they were, he would communicate with Mr. Bolton, who, he told them, was with the friendly Woolwa Indians. He told them to have no fear, but to go back at once, for to escape by flying through the woods was impossible. As the black spoke the shouts of their pursuers coming nearer was heard.

"In three or four days," said Cato, hurriedly, "you shall be free," and darted off into the wood.

"Come, Mary, let us thank God for this good news. I have no fear now," said Alice, "Mr. Bolton is on our track."

Holding Mary by the arm, Alice and her companion walked calmly out of the wood towards the hut, as Saunders and one of his associates, half drunk, came, out of breath, upon them. Seeing them quietly returning, Saunders paused, uttering a terrible malediction.

"How is this!" he exclaimed. "What made you leave the hut—were you trying to escape?"

"It does not look like it," said Alice, haughtily. "You see us going back. Fresh air and a little exercise is requisite, if you do not want to murder us by confinement."

"Curse you, you won't gammon me that way," said Saunders, reeling, as he made a grasp at Mary Pearson's arm, and held her by main force, despite her struggle. "Come, my beauty, I'll have you for a wife this night at all events."

But Mary Pearson, frantic with passion, suddenly snatched the long Mexican knife he wore in his belt, and, with all her force, drove it right at his breast. The steel buckle turned the blow, but, nevertheless, inflicted so severe a gash across his right breast, that the ruffian staggered and fell, believing, at first, that he was mortally wounded.

By this time the maidens were surrounded by a crowd of drunken Sambos, both men and women. One of the Mexican desperadoes drew a pistol and, with a frightful imprecation, swore, if Mary did not throw down the knife, he would shoot her. Alice, pale but collected, whispered some words to Mary, who at once threw the knife away, just as Saunders staggered to his feet and, pressing his hand to his chest, said:—

"You thought to murder me, you vixen. You have only scratched me, however; but you shall live, both of you, long enough to curse your existence. Take them," he continued, addressing the crowd, "and confine them in the stone-house, and manacle them with the chains. To-morrow I shall get over this scratch, and the schooner will be here, and then you will learn how William Saunders revenges himself on those he hates."

He became so weak from loss of blood, that he sank down on the ground, telling his comrades to get a bandage to stop the blood.

Six or eight Sambos then surrounded the two maidens, and seizing them by the arms, hurried them along towards the beach. At some distance from the huts stood a stone building, formerly belonging to some Prussians, who had settled on the musquito coast, but who had finally perished from the climate and the inhospitality and brutality of the Sambo negroes. This building was evidently used as a store—it had one strong, iron studded door, and a window twenty feet from the ground. At this time it was half unroofed by time and by storms—there was no kind of furniture in it—and into this miserable abode Alice and her unfortunate attendant were thrust, to pass the remainder of the night on the bare damp ground.

From a belt of trees Cato, the negro, was watching all that took place, and having seen them locked up in the building, he muttered:

"Ah, Ja, dat just do. Cuss him—dat berry fine girl—tam him, wish she had killed him;" and then, tightening his belt, he set out for the Woolwa Indian village.

Alice Marchmont, as soon as the door was closed and locked, and the vile rabble of men and women gone, threw herself into Mary's arms, and wept for several minutes unrestrainedly, the excitement of the last hour having completely overpowered her. Mary, equally excited, and tremblingly alive to the terrible scene they had gone through, still strove to soothe her mistress.

"Ah," said she, "if I had only killed the wretch! unfortunately, something broke or turned my blow; at all events the monster has a wound that will keep him quiet for a few days, and, before long, we shall, please God, be rescued."

"Wretch as that Saunders is, dear Mary, I am glad you did not kill him; the thought of having shed his blood and slain him would have haunted you through life."

"No, no," said Mary, resolutely, "to put out of the world such a monster, could create no other feeling than thankfulness that God had given me the power to do so. But what a wretched place the villains have put us in."

The moon had risen, and its rays shed a light through the broken roof, upon the shattered rafters and slates covering the stone floor. Seating themselves upon a block of stone, and leaning their backs against the wall, Alice, the child, we may say, of luxury, and her faithful attendant, passed the remaining hours of the night. Sleep was out of the question, for even within the dreary, bare, damp walls of the building the insatiable mosquitoes abounded, for that swampy shore was teeming with tropical insects of every description, whilst in the interior the Mexican lion, and various wild beasts roamed the vast forests unmolested.

Leaving our unfortunate heroine in her miserable prison, with her devoted attendant, we will, in our next chapter follow Mrs. Marchmont to Bluefields, and see what steps the fond mother took to rescue her lost daughter.

CHAPTER V.

Mrs. Marchmont, her daughter, and attendant, with most of their private effects, were embarked on board the Guarda Costa. In vain the fond mother strove to conceal the anguish of mind she experienced. In leaving the brig it appeared to her as if she were abandoning her child. Her daughter and old attached servant did and said all they could to cheer her, and persuade her that Alice would be restored to her safe and uninjured. Mrs. Marchmont was distressed too, by the unaccountable disappearance of Arthur Bolton and Joseph, at a time when their services would have been so valuable in rescuing her daughter from her abductors.

She resolved immediately on reaching Bluefields, to despatch some small vessel to Jamaica, with letters to her husband, entreating him to come to her, for to leave the musquito coast without positive intelligence of her daughter, was out of the question.

The captain of the Guarda Costa was civil and obliging enough, but understanding each other's language only imperfectly, little was said.

With a fair breeze, the Maria Gloriosa came in sight of Bluefields early on the following day. Mother and daughter were on deck, for the small, ill-ventilated cabin of the Guarda Costa was close and suffocating, and both gazed with a saddened feeling upon the long, white line of sand dividing the lagoon, on whose shores Bluefields stands, from the sea.

No scenery could be more monotonous or uninteresting. Here and there a solitary palm was to be seen, and a green belt of trees, and in the far distance the blue hills from which it takes its name.

As the Guarda Costa tacked, so as to run in through the narrow entrance, they had a clear view of the lagoon, at the extremity of which the town—if a collection of miserable huts could be called a town—stood, some ten miles distant from the entrance. No vessel of any country was to be seen upon that solitary sea, and within the lagoon, nought but patpans, and dories, and canoes were visible.

"What a wretched place," said Miss Marchmont to her mother, as the cutter ran swiftly up the lagoon, tacking here and there to avoid the many shoals scattered through its shallow waters.

"And yet," said the mother sadly, "Bluefields is called an imperial city, for that farce of a musquito king resides here."

"Oh, my dear mother!" said Miss Marchmont, incredulously. "A King—a black

King—and his palace is yonder wretched place."

"Your father, my dear girl, has often amused me with stories of these people and their king. When he was here there was an English resident; I forget his name, and the Musquito King resided with him. There was also a colony of Prussians, but somehow they all died, or vanished; indeed, your father said only five or six escaped out of a hundred or more. This climate and place is pestiferous, low, swampy, and intensely hot, subject to terrible storms and heavy rains; but see, the aspect of the town itself is picturesque," for amongst the huts they could see many palms and plaintain trees, and stalks of the golden fruited papayas. The entire shore seemed lined with dories, canoes, or patpans—many of the dories were from 50 to 60 feet long.

"But why are those people called Sambos?" questioned Miss Marchmont, "I thought they were all called mosquito Indians."

"There are Indian tribes in the interior," said Mrs. Marchmont, "some of them friendly, kind, and hospitable, but the race inhabiting the sea coast are a miserably degenerate brutal tribe; in fact, negroes or mongrels, half Indian and half negro, called Sambos."

The anchor was now let go, and the cutter's sail furled. Numerous canoes and patpans kept paddling round the vessel. One of them came along side with rather a singular person aboard—a hideous negro, dressed in a Post Captain's old tattered uniform, and calling himself an admiral. This negro could speak English. The Captain of the Guarda Costa permitted him to come aboard, and held him in conversation for some minutes; he then approached Mrs. Marchmont, making a tremendous bow, saying, "Morning, Mam."

Captain Castinos intimated to Mrs. Marchmont that this man had the command of the town during the absence of the King, and the English resident, who was daily expected to return from Jamaica—that he would order a hut to be prepared for him and his family, and recommended that she should bargain with him.

Mrs. Marchmont cared little about bargaining. She felt sorely depressed at hearing that the English resident was absent, and that there was not a single vessel of any description in the lagoon capable of going to Jamaica.

She told the Admiral she wanted for herself and family the best accommodation the place afforded; the terms were indifferent to her, but she must have a residence completely to herself.

The negro Admiral bowed profoundly and said: "Madame should ab de King's palace till de King comes back, and den she should ab anoder." He then summoned a dorie, and having again had a conference with the Captain of the Maria Gloriosa, Mrs. Marchmont's effects were brought on deck and lowered into the dorie, and then she and her daughter and attendants, after thanking Captain Castinos and distributing some dollars amongst the crew, entered the dorie, followed by the admiral, and four hideous negros paddled them ashore.

On reaching the landing place a great crowd attended, regarding our voyagers with much curiosity; but the admiral, who assumed airs of considerable importance, soon dispersed them, and, leading the way, ordered numerous negroes to carry the luggage.

The dwelling inhabited by the Musquito king and the English resident, was a small framed, plain-looking edifice, one story high, and divided into four chambers, most scantily supplied with very plain furniture. But Mrs. Marchmont and her daughter cared very little about their style of residence; they settled with the admiral to supply them with the best food the place afforded, and gave him some dollars to pay the negroes who carried their effects.

On talking to him about sending people in pursuit of the ruffians, who carried off her daughter, the admiral shook his woolly head, saying:

"The King and the English guvenor, would be home in two or three days, and den he would do all he could in de business."

This was all the answer Mrs. Marchmont could get, and it left her in a state of intense uneasiness. Her sole hopes now rested on Arthur Bolton, should he return to the brig, and on the exertions of the black cook, Cato.

Day after day the fond and anxious mother and sister watched for the English schooner from Jamaica; but not a sail threw a shadow on the still waters of the lagoon. They did not attempt to stir out of the hut, for the place was disgustingly filthy, and swarmed, like all Sambo villages, with naked children, pigs, and dogs.

On the tenth day of their residence, loud shouting, firing of guns, and sundry strange noises anounced some event, and shortly after the admiral made his appearance, announcing that the English schooner, with the King and Prime Minister was working up the lagoon.

Mrs. Marchmont, uttering the words, "Thank God, at last!" rushed to the window that looked down the lagoon, and beheld a handsome full rigged schooner with all sails set, tacking up the river. As the vessel neared the anchorage, the negroes began firing old rusty muskets, and a dilapidated old four-pounder, mounted on a platform some eight feet square, just before the house, was loaded, and after a variety of attempts fired, amidst a tremendous noise, shouts, cries, &c. No gun was fired from the schooner, and no flag displayed beyond the simple ensign flying at the peak. So the admiral informed Mrs. Marchmont, that the King could not be aboard, as his Majesty delighted in making much noise with guns and cannons.

As soon as the schooner anchored, her sails were furled, and her boats launched from her deck.

"I trust," said Mrs. Marchmont, to her

anxious daughter; "that though the King is not on board, the English resident is."

"We shall soon see, dear mother," returned Eliza Marchmont, "for there are several persons getting into the boats; but it is too far to distinguish figures. They are Europeans, at all events. There are four in the first boat."

Nearly all the population of the place rushed down to the beach, and surrounded the persons landing, and shortly they were lost to view.

After a few minutes, both mother and daughter perceived a single gentleman advancing rapidly towards the house they occupied.

Mrs. Marchmont gazed intently at the approaching figure, and then uttered an exclamation of joy:

"Oh, my child!" she exclaimed, clasping her hands, and tears streaming down her cheeks; "it is your father!"

Miss Marchmont rushed to the door; the

next moment, mother and daughter were folded in the arms of Mr. Marchmont. For some time not one of the party could speak, but gazed at each other with fond affection.

"Oh, William, my beloved husband! what an unexpected joy is this. Must I damp it by telling you—"

"Alas! I know all, my beloved Fanny. It was the first intelligence I heard on landing. I did not expect to find you and my child Eliza here. I only knew that the Foam was wrecked, or supposed to be wrecked, somewhere on the coast. So I at once, in terrible anxiety of mind, embarked with Captain Courtney."

"Captain Courtney!" exclaimed mother and daughter in a tone of bewildered amazement. "Surely, not poor Captain Courtney?"

"Yes, dear Fanny; it is the worthy Captain of the Foam I mean—most providentially saved, when cast overboard by those atrocious mutineers. I would not allow him to come with me till I broke the intelligence to you both. We have just heard from the negro, Admiral Wellington, that the Foam is safe, though dismasted, in the Punza Pulka river, and that the Maria Gloriosa is with her, getting up jury masts, &c. I will despatch twenty armed negros and six English sailors, with the dawn, to scour the country for those villains who hold my daughter's person; and to-morrow, I intend sailing in the schooner for the Punza Pulka river, and try and track them up that river. But where is Mr. Bolton? Captain Courtney is most anxious about him; Admiral Wellington knows nothing about him. But stay, I must go for Courtney, for he is very desirous to see you both."

"Oh, if our beloved Alice were but here!" exclaimed Mrs. Marchmont, clasping her hands, "what joy would be mine."

"God has been most merciful in his goodness," said Mr. Marchmont, with solemn earnestness, "may His mercy restore our child uninjured."

Mr. Marchmont then hurried to the hut, where he had left Captain Courtney.

"Oh, Eliza, I am so bewildered, so overpowered, and so thankful to Providence, that I scarcely know what I say or do."

"Only to think of Captain Courtney being alive! it appears incredible. There must have been some vessel near us on that dreadful night," said Miss Marchmont, "which picked him up."

"If that had been the case, my child, surely they would have pursued us; and besides, if so near, they must have heard the shouts and cries of the poor doomed steward, for he was not saved. But here comes your father, and our dear, good friend, the captain, looking as well as ever."

Captain Courtney was flushed and excited as he clasped Mrs. Marchmont's hand in both his.

"I cannot tell you, my dear madam," he exclaimed, with much emotion, "what joy this interview gives me, to see you and your daughters—for we will, please God, soon restore Miss Alice to your arms—safe. In the hour of my terrible trial, when death stared me in the face, I thought of you all, in the power of those remorseless ruffians."

Mrs. Marchmont shed a flood of tears; the memory of that hour, and the loss of her daughter, though hope was not dead in her heart, overpowered her. In the evening, when all were more calm and collected, and the heat of the day tempered by the cool breeze from the mountains, Captain Courtney gave the party assembled an account of his most providential escape from a terrible death.

"On that fearful night," began the captain, "when Mr. Bolton and I were seated conversing in my private cabin, the door was suddenly burst open, and Saunders and the others, after a desperate resistance from that gallant gentleman, Mr. Bolton, who was knocked down senseless, and would instantly have been murdered, had not my first mate, whose life, you may remember, he saved, interfered, overpowered us, dragged me up the cabin stairs—two or three of the ruffians making every effort to stab me with their knives, but in the confusion and darkness I fortunately escaped their blows, and was finally hoisted overboard—the craft then going at eight knots, but not much sea. The poor steward had fallen a victim to their brutal fury before, being thrown into the sea.

"My first thought was to recommend my soul to my Maker, and let myself sink, and thus end my misery. But I was always an excellent swimmer, aud somehow, strange as it may appear, the love of life prevailed, and I rose to the surface, and got rid of my coat, waistcoat, and shoes, and then turned on my back, and began, even in that terrible situation, to think. I thought of you all left in the power of those terrible villains; I thought of my home, of my dear wife and children, and then I prayed, feeling that before long I must sink. It was a very dark night, and as

I thus lay, rising and falling on the seas, my head came suddenly against something hard, and to save myself from sinking, as I was turned over on my face, I grasped at a mass of ropes in which I became entangled, and then I perceived even in the deep gloom, that I was holding on by the rigging tossed over an immense mast, and above me were the huge tops of a large ship. On to this mast I scrambled, and then up into the tops, which floated quite clear of the water. Here I paused to breathe, with a thanksgiving to Providence. I was saved for the time. Some ship might pass, might see me—there was a chance, and when will not man hope against the most desperate odds. I was now secure from drowning, for in the huge tops of a large ship, I was safe, even in a hurricane. Fastening myself round the waist, before morning I actually dozed.

"As the dull light of a gloomy day broke over the heaving ocean, I eagerly gazed around me; the weather foretold a storm, but no vessel was in sight. As I looked down, floating amongst the rigging, and held to the tops by a rope. I beheld the dead body of a man, a sailor by his dress, but fearfully decomposed. I shuddered as I cast off the rope to rid myself of a sight so sad. That poor wretch no doubt held on till starvation sapped life ; several others might have shared the same fate, and their fate, I thought, might be mine.

"The day passed, I lashed myself securely, for I saw by the look of the heavens that a storm was at hand, and that night it broke with surprising fury. It was only of a few hours' duration, and for half the time I was under water; but with daylight came blessed hope, for scarcely four miles from me, I beheld a large bark, under close-reefed canvas, running right for the heaving mast. I was, providentially, right in the ship's course. As the ship neared me they perceived the mast, and, standing up, I waved my arm, and shouted till I was hoarse. I was seen, and then it was that nature gave way, and, bursting into tears, I became insensible.

"When I recovered, I was in the ship's boat, the gallant fellows, though it was a work of great peril, having rescued me. The ship was Spanish, and bound to Cuba; the captain spoke French, and was most kind. He supplied me with garments, and shared his cabin with me, when I told him my story. A very heavy gale, in which he sprang his fore-topmast, and also sprang a leak, forced him to run for Jamaica, to my infinite joy, as I thought it possible some British cruizer would be induced to search for the brig and the mutineers; for I had a very good idea as to where they would run the Foam to plunder her. I knew that the second mate, Saunders, had once been on the musquito coast, and had often heard him talk of his wild course there, and how easy a fellow might lead a life of plunder, with the jolly lot of Mexican adventurers, who frequented that coast; but my first task, and that a most painful and dreaded one, was to find out Mr. Marchmont, and make him acquainted with my terrible story. I need not tell you or speak of that painful interview; you are now, thank God, united.

"Imagine my delight when, a few days after my arrival in Jamaica, a schooner cast anchor in the harbour, and reported that she spoke a Spanish Guarda Costa off the Punza Pulka river, on the Musquito coast, the captain of which stated that there was a large English brig ashore, dismasted in that river, and that he was going to Bluefields for assistance. The Governor at once placed a small armed schooner at Mr. Marchmont's service. We accordingly embarked with the English resident of Bluefields, and put in here to land him, intending to proceed to the Punza Pulka. Imagine our joy when the Negro Admiral told us you were here, but that one of your daughters had been carried off by a party of Sambos and some Mexican desperadoes. Such, my dear madam, is my brief narrative, which plainly shows that even in the most desperate circumstances we should never despair of the divine mercy and assistance of Providence."

CHAPTER VI.

The following morning beheld the departure of the schooner, with Mr. Marchmont, Captain Courtney, and a strong, armed party, for the Punza Pulka river. It was the most expeditious mode of proceeding. On reaching the brig, Mr. Marchmont, with negro guides, and a dozen well-armed sailors, and twenty armed negroes, sent by the English resident at Bluefields, to assist, proceeded to visit Quamwatta and all the Sambo villages on the different lagoons, till they discovered Miss Alice Marchmont, and rescued her.

They also took materials with them to complete the rigging of the Foam, to enable them to take her to Jamaica, calling off Bluefields for Mrs Marchmont and family.

Leaving them to prosecute their search, we return to our hero, whom we left in the village of the Woolwa Indians.

Arthur Bolton, in his intense desire to commence his search for Alice Marchmont, was up with the dawn; but the whole village was astir, and the chief, Punka Bósswash, was coming to his hut to rouse him, accompanied by a negro, attired in European costume, in whom, to his infinite delight, our hero recognised Cato, the cook of the Guarda Costa.

"Ah! my good friend," said Arthur, grasping the cook's hand, "have you any good news? Have you discovered where the young lady is?"

"Yes, massa, me ab. Me good news and bad news."

Punka Bosswash then proposed that they should go inside the hut, and consult about what was best to be done.

Accordingly they all entered, and sat

down on the logs of wood. Punka Bosswash lit his pipe and took a whiff, and Arthur Bolton, who knew that the Woolwas, though a sober race, loved a small allowance of brandy, produced his little jar, and handed a cup all round, and then begged Cato to tell his good news and bad.

Cato related how he thought he had tracked Miss Marchmont to Quamwatta, but before entering the village, he kept a secret watch upon what was going on; for he heard there was to be feasting for three days, and a "big drunk on the last day."

Whilst watching in the wood, he beheld, to his great surprise, two females, white people, leave a hut, and run into the wood, close by where he lay concealed. He at once knew that they must be Miss Marchmont and her attendant; he also knew it would be utterly impossible for them, even with his guidance, to escape through the forest, and across rapid streams, and their pursuers after them. So he advised them to go back, which they did, and then he continued his watch, and finally having seen Miss Marchmont and Mary forced into the stone house, which he described as a very strong place, with doors plated with iron; but with a rope ladder they could scale the walls, as half the roof was off.

Punka Bosswash listened to Cato's account with great attention, and, having finished his pipe, he said—"That's good," and then, nodding his head, told Cato to say what he thought it best to do.

Cato continued to say that, after quitting Quamwatta, he came up with two Sambos and two of their females; that he easily persuaded them that he was a runaway from the Spanish Guarda Costa, and was hiding in the forest till the schooner left the Punza Pulka. He had a full canteen of brandy, for on an emergency, he reckoned much upon its efficacy. Having primed the two Sambos and their wives, who belonged to Quamwatta, they told him if he went to their village he would be safe, for they had twenty Mexican desperadoes well armed, with them, and they would kill the men of the Guarda Costa if they came to their village. They also informed him that there was to be a "big drunk" for three days, and that a great "Sukia" (sorceress) was to be there, and that she was to defy fire, and to foretell the fortunes of the Mexicans who would come to the lagoon in their schooner, to take away their white wives, and go to Cape Gracias, to where gold was to be got, and where no power could touch them.

Arthur Bolton felt his cheeks flush as he heard this intelligence.

"Then," said he, "there is no time to be lost."

"No, massa, no time; cause to-morrow night last night of big drunk and the Sukia woman; they will den be all drunk, de men and de womens."

Punka Bosswash said he would collect twenty braves, all of their village—there was no time to send and collect more—but that before they tried force they should endeavour to get the women out over the walls of the great stone house. Everyone would be sure to be collected round the Sukia, to see her defy fire, and tell fortunes, and all were sure to be dead drunk after seeing her. They could easily lie concealed in the thick jungle at the back of the village.

This plan our hero approved, and forthwith Punka Bosswash proceeded to collect his twenty braves, and to have ladders of twisted grass made. The whole party was to set out at sunset, so as to reach Quamwatta by sunset the following night.

Our hero and Joe set about cleaning and preparing their arms. To Cato was given the carbine, and Joe took the cook's pistol.

By sunset three canoes were ready, and all the women of the village came to see them depart. Achupa was presented by Arthur Bolton with the only ornament he possessed, and that was a handsome gold ring. Dollars she refused, shaking her head, but the ring she hung round her neck, fastened to an Indian necklace, and bade our hero farewell with a somewhat sad smile.

It was our hero's intention to seize the Mexican schooner, and, putting Miss Marchmont and Mary Pearson on board, to sail for Bluefields, Cato knowing the coast well. Punka Bosswash was armed with an English musket, and his braves with bows and spears.

Proceeding down the Bosswash river they arrived, just as it became intensely dark, at the Rio Grande, and, crossing it to the eastward, stopped on the opposite shore for the remainder of the night. Fires were lighted to smoke away their bitterest enemies, the musquitoes; but the frightful noises, particularly those of the howling monkeys, that infested the great forest, quite banished sleep from Arthur Bolton's eyes. Besides, he felt such deep interest in the fate of Alice Marchmont and her faithful Mary, dreading lest Saunders and his villanous associates should carry them off before they could reach the stone house.

At this period the rainy season, always accompanied by storms, was expected, and when it does rain on the musquito coast, it is a ceaseless down-pour for days. Then swamp fevers rage with violence.

"No doubt," thought Arthur Bolton, "those ruffians, the Mexicans, will depart from this coast as soon as possible, for none but the natives have a chance of escaping the fever."

Thus he lay thinking through the hours of the night, the fires, notwithstanding the heat, being kept up to scare the musquitoes. Of wild beasts there was no fear, being so near the sea coast.

As soon as daylight appeared, the Indians prepared their food, and hauled up their canoes, as the rest of the journey was over land and through thick forests, so as not to cross any open country till they came to the borders of the lagoon on whose shores was the Sambo village of Quamwatta.

Punka Bosswash came and sat down by Arthur Bolton to smoke his pipe before starting. Our hero was making his breakfast off a fine fowl Joe had skilfully broiled.

"We shall reach the forest that backs the Sambo town of Quamwatta, by sun set," said Punka Bosswash, in his peculiar, but easily understood English; "and there we must lie hid till the great drink begins, for our force is small, and we should fail if we attacked them and the Mexican robbers before they all get drunk. You understand, my son."

"Yes, chief, I do," returned our hero. "I think only of the whites, those Mexican ruffians. The Sambos are great cowards; twenty brave Woolwas would drive into flight the whole village."

"The Woolwas are brave," returned the chief thoughtfully, "but they are prudent and wise. If the maidens can be carried off without surprising or alarming the Sambos or the Mexicans, so much the better."

To this our hero agreed, but should cunning not succeed, would the Woolwas fight to gain their object? asked Arthur.

"The Woolwas die," said the chief, proudly; "they never run, so be satisfied, we will free the maidens or fall."

Arthur pressed the chief's hand, and having finished his pipe, Punka Bosswash rose up, stating it was time to commence the journey. In ten minutes the Indians were all ready for the march, and our hero and Joe followed. Their way lay through a dense forest without any visible track; nevertheless the Indians knew well the direction to take; cutting through many obstacles and keeping steadily in one direction.

The overgrown and entangled vegetation under the deep shade of the trees, was to our hero wonderful to look at. Cato amused him telling him various stories of the Sambos, of their brutal love of intoxication, and the frightful excesses they committed when drunk, but even Cato, though many years a cook on board British ships, was a firm believer in the sorceries of the "Sukia," or fire woman. "De talk," said he, "and stand in de middle of a big wood fire till the cloth de hab round de loins do crisp and cut up, and de Sukia no feel de fire one bit."

"Well, Cato, that will not prove the miserable pretender, or sorceress, to be a witch, or able to work miracles. We have showmen and conjurers in England who can do the same for the small charge of one shilling. They wash their hands and feet or the whole body in the juice of some plants, or with some chemical preparation which resists fire, and I have no doubt your sorceress, the Sukia, does the same."

"Ja, ja, massa," returned Cato; "dat not so, de Sukia tell what come to-morrow. Cure de sick of de fever."

"I thoroughly suspect, Cato, that the cures

are very few compared to the deaths, for notwithstanding your famous Sukias, the race of the Sambos is yearly becoming less numerous and more sickly and weak."

"Ah, ja, massa, de drink till all blue—dat kill more den de fever, and we are not far from de rivers, and den come de fevers—de rivers rise—ten, twelve feet, and no possible pass across the country."

"If we can manage to get possession of the schooner, we can reach Bluefields much sooner and much easier than over land, so that if the rains do come on, they will not retard or interrupt our journey. You and I and Joe can easily work the little schooner to Bluefields."

"Ja, massy, easily. If we got over de bar at mouth of lagoon—it very bad bar—full of rocks and banks. De Guarda Costa nigh lost dere one fine night; if bad night, she sure go pieces."

Arthur felt uneasy; this was a contingency he had not taken into consideration, for even if they got the captives to the shelter of the schooner, and afterwards ran aground on the bar, the Sambos would surely pursue them in canoes and patpans, and if recaptured he shuddered to think what might be their fate. During the journey, though his mind was preoccupied, still he could not but observe the wild, and at times, singularly picturesque scenery they passed through; with his gun he could have killed abundance of game; amid the dense coverts of the jungle bounded the antelope and the deer. Numbers of gibionite and the cani-paca or pig rabbit, scampered over the Savanna, and here and there that magnificent bird, the crested carrassow, walking with stately step, showing but little fear at the approach of man; innumerable quails, also invited the sportsman, so little afraid were they of an enemy. Night and morning also the air was filled with cries of the chattering of parrots and macaws. Our hero felt a great wish to bring down a carrassow, its plumage so beautiful and as large as a turkey; the rich dark brown of its feathers, except on the neck, where the colors became ash, and the breast a reddish brown.

On leaving the forest, they came to a most magnificent savannah, though of limited extent, through which ran a shallow river; along the bank of this river the scenery was exceedingly beautiful. Giant cestas, the feathery palm, and the singular trunks of the matapato, so much resembling snakes as to startle the traveller; round these, hundreds of beautiful plants bound their slender tendrils, and here and there in clumps of gorgeous colours—flowering with a splendour known only in tropical climes—the astonishing variety of acacias, the fine-leaved gum arabic, palmathos, and mixed with them, dark groups of pines, and though all so various in their colours and shades, Nature had grouped them so harmoniously, that no disorder appeared in the arrangement.

" What a lovely spot—and what scenery," thought Arthur Bolton; "and yet what a deadly climate—death and beauty hand-in-hand!"

During the day's journey they saw many snakes, some very large, but only one poisonous; and one of the Indians narrowly escaped its bite; stooping to pick up a branch under which was coiled what the Musquitoes call the pinta sura, poison snake; it struck at him, but by great good fortune missed its aim—he then killed it. This snake was not more than twenty-six inches long, and not thicker than a man's thumb, with a somewhat large flat head. The Indians consider it one of the most deadly under the tropics.

It wanted an hour of sunset, when the party entered the dense wood that extended to the back of the Quamwatta village, and still at some distance.

Avoiding all possible tracks made by the Sambos, they pushed their way through almost impenetrable masses of jungle and underwood, till just as it grew dark, the party halted; by this time the howling monkey had commenced his nocturnal music, and the noise was deafening.

"Cuss des customers," said Cato, as he joined our hero; "de make de debbles noise."

"What is to be done now, Cato?" demanded our hero, as Punka Bosswash sat down and was surrounded by his braves.

"You come wid me, massa, and I take you to a place where you will see what's going on in the village; you will see where missy is kept shut up, and when all get well drunk, we will carry off missy to the schooner, if she is there."

To this our hero eagerly agreed, and Punka Bosswash and his braves, after a short consultation with Arthur Bolton, also proceeded to a place where they could inspect the proceedings in the village. They had scarcely traversed half a mile towards their intended place of concealment, when the shouts and cries from the Sambo village reached their ears. Cato led the way; and presently the light from the fires flashed through the trees.

They then separated, and our hero, with Cato and Joe, crept up so close to the village that they could distinctly observe the faces of those collected in crowds, and yet remain perfectly concealed in the thick growth of low shrubs that covered a ridge of sand, about two hundred yards from the waters of the lagoon, and scarcely six from the scene of the festivities.

We may readily imagine the feelings of our hero, as lying flat upon the ground, he gazed out from the thick cover upon the scene before him. The village of Quamwatta consisted of an irregular row of miserable huts, on a slightly rising ground above the broad lagoon. A great crowd of Sambos men, women, and children were collected together in groups, and shouting, dancing, and vociferating furiously, the whole scene lighted up by numerous torches stuck in the ground, and here and there great fires. The stone house Arthur Bolton eagerly looked for, and Cato pointed it out to him. It was some distance from the village, and close to the borders of the lagoon.

Cato, in a low voice, said: "The schooner is at anchor. I see de masts."

Our hero looked, and at length made out the little vessel some three-quarters of a mile below the stone building,

Cato then pointed out the canoe where the great drink, the mushla, was prepared. This beverage is composed of pine apples, plaintains, cassava, and maize. These compounds being bruized, are thrown into a canoe, water added, and then Indian corn masticated by the chiefs' wives and daughters, and the whole stirred up with a big stick or one of their canoe paddles, and then the assembled crowd surround the canoe with shouts and cries and extraordinary gestures and contortions, and antics, and dipping in their cocoa nuts, drink till the scene becomes too disgusting to describe.

As our hero watched anxiously what was going on, he beheld a party of Mexicans come out of a large hut; all had fire arms, and as they passed on into the crowd of women, he distinctly recognised Will Saunders. The cries and shouts became loud and furious, as men and women began imbibing the contents of the canoe, the Mexicans joining and firing off their guns, to the frantic delight of the Sambo women, who commenced dancing. Presently a great fire was made, and when it blazed up a crowd of women came forth from a hut, surrounding a woman with no other covering than a narrow long cloth. The Mexicans, with Saunders, also joined the group, and all ranged themselves in rows on three sides of the fire. Cato touched our hero, saying: "The Sukia woman; after her performance, they will all get frightfully drunk. We must then break into the stone house, and as soon as we can release the prisoners, get to the schooner; the wind blows out of the lagoon, but the weather looks bad."

Bolton was so intent watching the proceedings before the hut that he paid no attention to the weather, which looked dark and lowering over head. As the Sukia woman approached the fire, the Mexicans and Will Saunders handed her something which she laid on the ground. She then calmly and quietly stepped into the midst of the flaming pile; there was no deception. Arthur Bolton certainly beheld her with exceeding surprise. She was a tall thin woman, straight and erect, and as she stood unmoved, the flames darted up and encircled her above the waist and even to the head. She was perfectly nude save the thin torrison. She appeared like a statue till the blaze fell. She broke a bamboo staff and from it took a large Tamagasa snake, which she grasped, went through some ceremonies, which our hero could not distinctly see, and finally trampling out the flames, she walked up to the Mexicans, and waving her arms in a strange manner, no doubt predicted their future destinies, whatever they might be. Then commenced a scene of drinking and abominable orgies, till men and women fell down drunk, shouting furiously and beating drums, whilst every available noise a brutal population could make rent the air.

"Now, massa, let us go," said Cato; "we break into de house. De chief and his young men watch and keep de drunken Sambos away if they see us."

Disgusted and eager to release his beloved Alice from her miserable prison, Arthur sprang to his feet, and he and Joe looking to see that their arms were all right, followed Cato through the wood. Punka Bosswash saying he and his young men would keep between them and the village, and keep back the Sambos till they saw them embark in the schooner. One of his young men, Punka Bosswash observed, had examined the schooner from the shore, and there were only two men on board.

Keeping a bank of bushes between them and the shore of the lagoon, our hero and his two attendants reached to within fifty yards of the stone building, when the noise of oars in the water startled them, and they paused, crouching down behind the bushes; the night was exceedingly dark, but the lights from the scene of festivity flashed against the high walls of the old stone house. It was necessary in approaching the prison of Alice Marchmont to be quick in their movements, for should any of the revellers happen to look in that direction, they could easily distinguish them. The fall of the oars came nearer, and at length they perceived the schooner's small boat with two Mexican sailors pulling, run ashore close to the house. The two men landed, threw a grapnell out to secure the boat, and then approached the door of the house and paused, and both spoke in their own language for some moments. One man moved on towards the village, the other hesitated, but at length joined his comrade, and both proceeded towards the scene of festivity.

"Ah, ja, dis very good," said Cato; "dere boat for go board schooner."

"What did they say, Cato?" questioned Arthur.

"One say, massa, to de oder, you go tell dem drinking that de tide soon turn de much sea on bar. De oder say, 'Come, comrade, we have half an hour's lark, and de both go.'"

"Then we must lose no more time, Cato. It's a dark night, and we must pass the bar. Have you the rope ladders, Joe?"

"Yes, sir, I have them." Then stooping as low as possible, they passed across the open space and reached the door of the house. A short examination convinced them of the impossibility of forcing the iron-bound doors. Passing round the house, Arthur examined the wall where the roof was broken in, and taking the rope prepared for the purpose, with a small grapnell at the end, he threw it over the wall, the hooks caught, and then proving the strength, Joe, being the lightest, quickly ascended, and hauling up the rope ladder, made it securely fast to a rafter, and then his master, with a beating heart, followed.

The noise, slight as it was, evidently alarmed those below, for a faint cry of alarm reached his ears as he threw down the ladder. Arthur quickly descended, saying in a low, clear voice: "Miss Marchmont—Alice—beloved Alice, it is I,—Arthur Bolton."

An exclamation of joy burst from the lips of the over-joyed girl, as she rushed towards the sound of his voice; in the impulse of the moment he clasped her to his heart with a feeling of love and devotion.

"Oh, Arthur," she exclaimed, as Mary Pearson, weeping with emotion, joined them. "This moment of joy repays me for all my sufferings; and my beloved mother and sister?"

"All well, thank God," said our hero, pressing the hand of poor Mary, who was beside herself with joy. "No time must be lost, Alice; you must try and mount this ladder."

As he said the words, Joe called out from above, "Make haste, sir; Cato says the Indians have given the alarm, and I see dark figures moving out from the crowd and coming this way.

Placing two heavy stones on the ropes to steady the slight ladder, Arthur Bolton ascended, taking the precaution to pass a rope round Alice's waist, so as to steady her, and in case of accident, should she slip. With a beating heart, but firm nerve, the young girl safely gained the top of the wall, followed by Mary Pearson, and then as quickly they gained the ground.

By this time a crowd of intoxicated Sambos, carrying torches, were rushing, screaming and shouting towards the house; the Mexicans and Sambos, dreadfully intoxicated staggering after. They caught sight of the fugitives as they ran towards the beach. Arthur Bolton, carrying Alice in his arms, and Cato catching up Mary like an infant, they made way rapidly for the boat. Suddenly Punka Bosswash and his braves, with the true Indian war cry, rushed upon the drunken Sambos, and in a minute the terrified wretches fled back to their huts; but Saunders and half a dozen Mexicans broke through and had reached within fifty yards of the fugitives, who were then close to the boat. Saunders and the Mexicans paused and fired, but providentially they were too drunk to aim accurately, and the balls rattled harmlessly by.

Placing Alice in the boat, Arthur seized his gun, and singling out Saunders, fired. The ruffian fell on his knees, but with a yell he regained his feet and ran on. By this time the boat was afloat, and Cato and Joe pulling out into the lagoon. Fortunately in their haste and drunkenness the Mexicans had forgotten their ammunition.. Punka Bosswash and his braves, seeing the boat afloat and the enemy baffled, gave a loud whoop of triumph and disappeared in the woods.

CHAPTER VII.

We have said in the preceding chapter that the weather towards the decline of day looked lowering and threatening. In fact the temporale was daily expected—a period of storms and tremendous rain, though of short duration.

So absorbed, however, were our adventurers in their projects that they paid little if any heed to the aspect of the heavens; but scarcely had our hero succeeded in getting Alice Marchmont and Mary into the boat and pulled out from the shore, than they were startled by a flash of vivid lightning, instantly followed by one of those tropical peals of thunder that must be heard to be appreciated, for the crash over their heads was more like the uprooting of a world than a thunder peal, so terrible, so prolonged did it appear.

Alice trembled and hid her face in her hands; the boat appeared to rock under them. Cato and Joe pulled manfully, whilst Arthur steered for the schooner, revealed to them distinctly by the continued flashes of lightning.

"Massa," said Cato, "dis berry bad. Wind gone. De cursed Mexicans run back for canoes to pursue us."

"Ah, Arthur, we shall be overtaken, and you will be slain!" cried Alice, in terror.

"Have no fear, dearest," whispered our hero; "lay your head on Mary's lap. She is a brave girl, with a stout heart. You are mine now, and only with life shall they separate us. This storm comes from the east, and the wind will rise. Ha! the schooner, lay in your oars."

A flash revealed, at that moment, every object distinctly for a long way. Our hero saw the schooner; and Cato and Joe beheld a dozen canoes in pursuit.

Scarcely were they along side, and Alice and Mary placed on board, ere the storm gust came sweeping down the lagoon, forcing the water from the surface and scattering it in drifts over the vessel, almost blinding those aboard, and, although the thunder ceased, down came the rain, with continuous blaze of lightning of the deepest blue, playing, as it were, over the surface of the lagoon, lingering upon the iron work of the schooner, and rendering every object as distinct and visible as open day.

Placing Alice and her attendant in the shelter of the little cabin—Cato and Joe began to cast off the lashings of the foresail, and to heave up the anchor—but a flash of vivid lightning revealed to our hero a dozen canoes and patpans within fifty yards of them.

"Cut away the cable, Cato," Bolton shouted to the black. "Joe, run up the foresail—the canoes are close along side."

Up went the foresail, and the schooner swung round with the fierce squall, just as a large patpan, full of Sambos and two or three Mexicans, ran against her, and were sunk. Two Mexicans made an effort to cling to the rigging, but our hero, with a blow on the head with the butt of Joe's carbine, dashed one into the boiling sea, while Cato, with a turtle spear, disposed of the other.

Away flew the schooner, Cato steering, by calling out to our hero at the helm, "starboard and then port," as they flew by some rock or bank, seen by the lightning flash; the shrieks and cries of the baffled Sambos and Mexicans, as they strove to regain the shore in the ruffled waters, were drowned in the whistling of the blast through the rigging. Fortunately the wind blew right out; still it required all Cato's watchfulness and knowledge to avoid the rocks that lay scattered over the entrance into the lagoon. The rain came down in a deluge, beating the decks of the little schooner like hail drops, and the furious blasts driving it with remorseless fury in the faces of the anxious crew. As they reached the bar, the great heave of the sea was felt, but, being partly off the land, the little vessel was able to bear the close reefed canvass. The open sea gained, Arthur proposed to the black cook to heave her to for the night, on account of the numerous keys (reefs) that lay some distance off from the land and extending for a considerable distance all along the Musquito Coast.

Having no great deal of sea to contend against, the schooner lay to very well. The lightning shortly after ceased, and the gale moderated; but the rain fell in one continued down pour. Shut up in the little suffocating cabin, the odour of turtle shells, stock-fish, and half-decayed gourds and melons, with which the lockers were stuffed, Alice Marchmont and Mary were nearly fainting when Arthur Bolton removed the hatch to give them air, as the sea no longer washed over them, and a tarpaulin to windward protected them from rain.

It was by this time near early dawn, and the clouds shewed symptoms of breaking, for the temporale on that coast had intervals of quiet, though, in general, the storms followed one another rapidly.

As the dawn made, Arthur anxiously gazed into the pale features of his beloved Alice.

"You have suffered, dear Alice," he said, pressing her small hand, tenderly; "suffered much, I fear."

"Yes, Arthur," said the young girl. "We have both suffered; but our bodily sufferings were nothing compared to our mental tortures. If you had not rescued us last night, I shudder to think what I might have been tempted to do; for we knew that wretch Saunders and his associates intended putting us aboard this vessel, and sail for some part of the coast, where we should perish a miserable death, for live to endure such degradation as was threatened us would be impossible; but for Mary's tenderness and devotion I should have given way to despair."

"And to think, after all," said Mary Pearson, bitterly, "that the miserable wretch, Saunders, should escape."

"His time will come, Mary; he will not escape the punishment due to his crimes, depend on it. I struck him when I fired, but did not wound him seriously, for he was up in pursuit the moment after."

"Now tell me of my beloved mother and sister," said Alice; "they must have suffered severely?"

"I have not seen them, dear Alice, since the day I boarded this schooner, for this is the same I swam to from the Foam."

"Good heaven! is it possible?" exclaimed Alice surprised. "Where have you been, and how came *you* so blessedly to our rescue?"

Arthur Bolton told her all, briefly stating his own adventures. By this time it was broad day-light; the rain had ceased, but the weather looked wild and stormy, with a shifting wind.

Cato came aft, and proposed their running into the Punza Pulka, where the Foam was sure to be, especially as he said there was not a morsel of food there that Missy could eat; and he looked, besides, for a gale from the westward, against which they could never work to Bluefields.

Though Alice, pale, exhausted, and really unwell, anxiously desired to reach Bluefields, to join her mother and sister; yet she saw the necessity of following Cato's advice, for it began to blow hard, and the sea to rise, so, close reefing their sails, they began working to windward, and, having an ebb tide in their favour, they made the mouth of the Punza Pulka in three hours, and running in between the islands to smooth water, permitted Alice and her attendant to dispense with the hatches.

"Holly, golly! Massa!" exclaimed Cato,

"dare be the ship in the river—the Guarda Costa, and an English schooner."

All aboard the little vessel turned their eyes in the direction of the Foam, and to Arthur Bolton's great surprise he beheld the brig with jury masts up, and her rigging and yards, though on a very small scale, nearly ready. Close beside her was a large schooner, with the long pennant streaming in the breeze, and, at a short distance, the Maria Gloriosa was at anchor.

"Ah!" said Alice Marchmont, with a slight tinge of her former colour in her cheeks, and her fine eyes sparkling with pleasure, "there is the dear old brig with its masts up. Who can they be in that English vessel? Who do you think, Arthur?"

"Most likely she is from Bluefields, and come to help the Guarda Costa to take the brig to Jamaica."

"Oh, if dear Captain Courtney and the poor little steward were alive, we could almost forget what we have gone through."

Cato got ready an anchor and cable as they ran up towards the Foam; their vessel was already perceived, and many persons were looking over the bulwarks, both of the brig and schooner; running up close to the cutter, Cato hauled down the sails and Joe let go the anchor.

The schooner's boat, with an officer in the stern-sheets, and a couple of seamen pulling, came along side the turtle schooner. The officer, jumping aboard, looked with exceeding surprise at Miss Marchmont, and then at our hero—raising his hat, he said, politely saluting Alice—"Miss Marchmont, I presume?"

Alice bowed, and then turning to Arthur Bolton, he said—"I suppose, sir, you are Mr. Bolton, who was passenger in the Foam, reported missing?" On our hero's replying in the affirmative, he continued. "You have been fortunate in rescuing Miss Marchmont. I am sure her father will be most rejoiced at your success, on his return."

"My father!" exclaimed Alice, clasping her hands, "has he been here?"

"Yes, Miss Marchmont, he has. He and Captain Courtney of the Foam."

Alice turned pale, and fell back against the hatchway, her dark eyes fixed on Lieutenant Staunton with a look of utter amazement—whilst our hero, though mystified, said:

"Can you mean Captain Courtney, who left England as the Captain of the Foam, and whom I saw thrown into the sea by his cowardly and mutinous seamen?"

"The same, Mr. Bolton," returned the Lieutenant; "he was singularly preserved, and is at this moment with Mr. Marchmont and a strong party, gone into the Sambo district to hunt out those rascally Mexican deserters. How you managed, with only that black and the young lad there, to rescue Miss Marchmont, appears to me marvellous."

"Oh, I had the assistance of a party of Woolwa Indians," returned our hero; "but, Miss Marchmont, you and Mary had better get on board the Foam, and occupy your old quarters till your father returns; you will find abundance of provisions."

"Anything Miss Marchmont or you may require," said Lieutenant Staunton, "you are welcome to out of my stores."

"You are very kind, sir," said Alice, "we will go at once."

By this time the Captain of the Guarda Costa had reached the side of the turtle schooner, and was receiving all the particulars of their seizing the craft, &c., from Cato.

Alice and her attendant were then put aboard the Foam, by the cutter's boat, and, after leaving the turtle schooner as a prize to the Maria Gloriosa, Arthur followed, promising Lieutenant Staunton to spend the evening with him.

Joe returned to the brig, and Cato, highly pleased and sure of being well rewarded by Mr. Marchmont, went back to the "Maria Gloriosa."

Alice Marchmont found everything untouched in her own and sister's private cabin, for Mrs. Marchmont had purposely left everything she thought she might want, when rescued from the miscreants who carried her off. She felt both weary and worn out from the suffering of mind and body she had endured, and the miserable treatment she had received. The two or three days passed in the damp, dismal, and totally unfurnished stone house, with only a scanty supply of dried grass to lie upon, and wretched food which she could scarcely bring herself to eat, was beginning to tell upon her constitution. Mary, more robust, and able to bear hardship, struggled against the suffering, aided by her ardent love for her young mistress.

Having made a cup of coffee, and obtained some slight refreshment, Mary persuaded Alice to retire to rest, saying: "one hour's rest with a mind free from care, would be worth all the sleep she had had from the period she left the Foam."

Alice's mind, however, was not free from

care or relieved from painful thought, though she knew her mother approved of her having bestowed her affection upon Arthur Bolton, and herself admired and esteemed the young man for the sterling qualities he possessed. She knew her mother secretly dreaded an explanation with Mr. Marchmont, for though a most kind husband and father, she was aware that he was a proud man, and ambitious of seeing his daughters well married. Wealth was not his object. Himself a younger branch of a noble family, and master of great wealth, he meditated, on his return to England, to mate his daughters with men of rank and high birth. Alice and her mother knew our hero's history, and doing so, they both felt apprehensions that the meeting with Mr. Marchmont might cruelly dissolve the happy dreams of the young lovers.

Arthur, now that the excitement was over, also had his misgivings, as to the reception he might meet with from Mr. Marchmont, when Alice would be restored to her father, principally through his courage and perseverance; but would that alone reconcile the wealthy merchant to give his beautiful and accomplished daughter to a man not only without fortune; but worse, actually without a name he could conscientiously lay claim to.

To drive away unpleasant thoughts, having seen that Alice had all she required, and Mary having told him she had persuaded her to take some hours' repose, he took a look at those setting up the rigging of the brig; they were most of them English sailors brought for that purpose from Jamaica. Though jury rigged, and hastily put up, yet the Foam was beginning to look ship shape; she had a quantity of stores in her and plenty of new sails, which, with a couple of reefs in them, would suit the jury yards tolerably well. He then proceeded to board the English schooner to spend the evening with Lieut. Staunton; he felt so amazed at the escape of Capt. Courtney, that he could scarcely think of anything else. The Lieutenant received him very kindly, for he was rather curious to hear all the particulars of the mutiny aboard the Foam and the abduction of Miss Marchmont. He had noticed the attachment of our hero and the fair Alice; in fact, he thought it could scarcely be otherwise, so fascinating and lovely did the lady appear.

Our hero, as they sat enjoying their wine and cigars, frankly told him all their adventures from the time they left England.

Lieut. Staunton was surprised, and so intimate and friendly did the two young men become, that they parted late that night with a feeling of sincere friendship.

The following morning Alice and our hero met at breakfast. As he pressed the fair hand held out to him, and gazed fondly into the sweet, pale, thoughtful face, he said:

"My own Alice, I fear you have suffered more than you choose to say. Oh! that I had that villain, Saunders, in my grasp."

"Better as it is, dear Arthur; better, far, that the God he has outraged should punish him, than his blood should be on your hands. I have been mercifully spared; and though a great sufferer, I have been providentially saved from greater evils. Let us think no more of the past, but look hopefully to the future. How miraculous was Captain Courtney's preservation! Does it not show, Arthur, that even in the most apparently helpless and desperate situation, there is a hand to save?"

"Your father, dear Alice, will no doubt return some time to-day, for he will hear of your rescue, either from some of the Woolwa Indians, or the Sambos of Quamwatta. I see the larder of the "Foam" requires some little dainty to be added to it. Lieut. Staunton says he will hasten the fitting out of the brig, so as to take advantage of this high spring tide, and get over the bar; so I and Joseph will take the small boat, and go up the river and kill you a few of the blue-winged teal. Some time ago you said you should like to have one of those beautiful macaws. I will catch you one if I can."

"Oh do not go ashore any more on this coast, dear Arthur; who can tell who may be prowling about, watching us."

"Depend on it, dearest, the ruffians are all dispersed, and far away by this time. The news of a strong party in pursuit of them, is sure to have reached and induced them to fly into the interior."

Still Alice begged him not to mind the macaw; so, kissing the fair hand held out to him, he promised to obey her wishes. Lovers' promises should never be broken; but we will not anticipate.

On ascending on deck with his fowling-piece, he called Joseph, and told him to get the small boat ready, as he was going to shoot a few teal and duck.

"I would go with you, Bolton," said Lieutenant Staunton, joining him, "but I promised Capt. Courtney to inspect and hurry the work aboard the brig. He did not like to let Mr. Marchmont go without his company. It is a fine day, but there will be another storm before twenty-four hours are over. You will be back to dinner?"

"Oh, yes; I shall only knock over a few teal; they keep farther away now the vessels are here, than they did; they soon learn to know an enemy."

"Will you take another hand with you?" asked the Lieutenant, as our hero and Joe pushed off.

"I thank you, no; there's plenty to do aboard. We shall float up with the tide, and come back when it turns."

Alice, from the cabin window, watched her lover, till the bold jutting promontory, half-a-mile up, shut him out from her view."

"It is very strange, Mary," said our heroine to her attendant, "but I feel dreadfully nervous, seeing Mr. Bolton go up the river to day; I have such a horror of the miscreants, we so blessedly escaped from, that I think they would sacrifice life, to be revenged upon him."

"Indeed, Miss Alice, I feel equally nervous; not that I think there can be the slightest risk to Mr. Bolton, whilst he stays in the boat; but he might just as well have remained aboard the brig."

"Why, you see, Mary, he is anxious to get me a few birds, as he is aware that there is nothing but salt meat aboard, and he knows I do not like it; but I trust our uneasiness may be nothing more than a feeling caused by our past sufferings."

Alice, nevertheless, continued uneasy, and watched the turning of the tide. Still no signs of her lover's return.

Lieutenant Staunton saw that Miss Marchmont was anxious, and with much kindness and good taste said, "I have no doubt Mr. Bolton has gone further up the creek than he intended, hoping to meet Mr. Marchmont and his party." This, Alice thought very probable.

Towards sunset, two boats were seen descending the river, before a strong gale which had sprung up; Lieutenant Staunton knew they were those belonging to Mr. Marchmont and Captain Courtney.

"Here comes your father, Miss Marchmont, and Captain Courtney, and no doubt Mr. Bolton is with them," said the Lieutenant, "for I see a small boat towing astern." But the sun was setting behind the forest-clad hill, and those in the boats were in the shade.

Alice had not seen her father for several years, therefore, with an anxious beating heart she hurried on deck. It was still light enough, when the boats came along-side, for the keen eyes of Alice Marchmont to perceive, that amongst the party, Arthur Bolton was not; she felt her heart sinking, and her limbs trembling under her. But her father sprang aboard, and, clasping her in his arms, kissed her fondly; but as he did so, she heard Lieutenant Staunton say to Captain Courtney

"Did not you meet Mr. Bolton? How came you with the dingy?"

"Arthur Bolton!" repeated the captain. "No! we came across the dingy, bottom up."

Alice heard no more, and when her father gently lifted her head from his shoulder, he perceived to his great astonishment that she had fainted. In a moment Captain Courtney guessed the cause; he, however, said nothing. More than one excitement he had no doubt had caused Miss Marchmont to faint. The anxious father carried her below, consigning her to the care of Mary Pearson, who placed her on the sofa in her own cabin.

In the meantime much alarm was felt by Captain Courtney and Lieutenant Staunton.

"Where did you find the dingy, Captain Courtney?" anxiously inquired Lieutenant Staunton. "It is now getting dark, and there is every appearance of a heavy gale, for already the gusts are violent."

"We picked up the boat, bottom up," said Captain Courtney. "I knew the dingy was yours, but I had no idea that any one had been using it. We imagined it had got adrift from you, and been upset somehow. It's being upset does not alarm me as to my young friend, Mr. Bolton, being drowned; he is a most splendid swimmer, and Joe, the lad, swims well. We did not look ashore, for we saw this storm brewing, and pulled vigorously back. My idea is they have landed to shoot something, and the boat got adrift and upset. By Jove ! it is beginning to blow tremendously, and the brig will float next tide."

"I would send a boat up along the opposite shore," said Lieutenant Staunton, "but no boat could make head way against this tide and gale, which looks as if it would increase to a hurricane."

And so it did; before twelve o'clock that night a furious tempest raged from the north-west, and the night was intensely dark. So tremendously did it blow, that when the brig floated, she was carried two miles below where she first ran a-ground, and with great difficulty was brought up; the Guarda Costa was driven ashore, and the English schooner narrowly escaped the same disaster.

When morning dawned, the gale continued so severe that no boat could make head against such wind and sea. As the bar had barely sufficient water for the brig to float over, should the wind continue in the same point, and the spring tides falling, Captain Courtney resolved to put to sea at once, the brig being quite ready. He would stand along the coast, he said, and anchor off Bluefields. The Guarda Costa was got off and put to sea, and deeply as it grieved him, Lieutenant Staunton was forced by his orders to keep with the brig, but Captain Courtney and Mr. Marchmont resolved to send out persons from Bluefields to traverse the country and endeavour to trace out the fate of Arthur Bolton and the boy Joseph.

CHAPTER VIII.

We have stated in one of our previous chapters that Sir Richard Morton's intention was to proceed to New York. He accordingly embarked, and after a tolerable passage of fourteen days, reached that city. Too anxious and too intent on accomplishing the object of his voyage to trouble himself with sightseeing, the following day he was on his way to Williamsburg, having disguised himself in the simple garb of a working artizan, looking out for a place to settle in. He then proceeded to Delawarr, and took up his abode at a small inn. The town, built upon the broad peninsula, formed by the confluence of the

Pamunky and Mattapone rivers, which, however, at this point are called the "York River," was a place of considerable size and importance; it would therefore not be very easy to discover where such a man as John Mason was located, and such Sir Richard found to be the case, and for several days he was baffled. Mason did not dwell in the town, of that he was soon convinced. At last he learned from a farrier, who chanced to put up with half-a-dozen horses at the same inn, that there was a man of the name of Mason, who farmed a track of land—swampy land it was for the most part—on the banks of the Mattapone river, some fifteen miles from Delawarr and dealt largely in horses, the farrier said.

"Was he a man much liked by those that knew him," questioned the disguised Baronet.

"Well, for my part," said the farrier, "I can only say what I hear, as I don't live nigh enough to him; I only goes for a spell at odd seasons. They do say as how they are a hard family to do with. When they came to these here parts, there was the father, mother, three sons and two daughters. Two of the sons were very young, and so was one daughter. The eldest daughter was married—"

"Married!" interrupted the Baronet, with a start, and a flush overspreading his face, which attracted the notice of the farrier, who was drinking some mint julip at the Baronet's expense.

"I guess, friend, you be interested in these Masons—or an old sweetheart of the girl's perhaps."

"Yes, friend, I am," returned Sir Richard, in considerable emotion, "though not the girl's sweetheart. I knew the Masons before they came to this country, therefore I am anxious to know how they get on. I intend going to see them."

"Well, friend," returned the man, "I'm of the old country; though twenty years knocking about these here parts has made almost a native of me. I'm going to-morrow, or the day next, within five miles of Mason's farm, and can give ye a lift to the Fork; and there's a rough road from there right away through the Swamp to his house."

To this the Baronet agreed with many thanks; he felt as if a mighty weight was taken off his mind. If Mason's daughter was married, it was clearly evident that the whole confession of Jay Pearson was a fabrication.

It then occurred to Sir Richard that it would be desirable to make inquiries whether the names of the two witnesses attached to the confession were in existence, or whether they ever existed.

After half an hour's thought, he determined to consult a professional man.

Having made inquiries, he heard of a gentleman of the name of Bowen, a Welshman, who bore an exceedingly good character, and who for five and twenty years had practised his profession of attorney, in Delawarr, and with considerable success. Having changed his clothes he proceeded to Mr. Bowen's residence, and had an interview with that gentleman.

Mr. Bowen was an elderly man, with very agreeable manners.

On requesting to know how he could serve his visitor, Sir Richard at once stated who he was, and that he had come from England for the express purpose of making enquiries concerning a family who had left England in the year 184—, and had settled either in Delawarr or its vicinity.

Mr. Bowen was a shrewd man of business; the title and distinguished appearance of his visitor induced him to pay special attention. He therefore replied: "Most probably he could give him the information he required, as he kept a record of events, and also a book of reference, respecting every settler from the mother country who visited and took up their residence in Delawarr or its immediate vicinity."

"The persons I seek are named Mason,—John Mason, the father."

"Dear me," interrupted the Attorney, "I know the family quite well; they occupy a farm called the Fork, upon the banks of the Potomy. They arrived,—let me see,"—and he took down a large folio with the date 184— on the back, and opened it. After turning over some pages, he read out: "John Mason and family—wife, three sons, and two daughters; wife since dead; aged about forty-eight or forty-nine."

"That's the family," interrupted Sir Richard. "Are the two daughters unmarried?"

"Well, I can tell you all about them, Sir Richard; but regret that I cannot say anything in their favour. The two sons are wild and fierce fellows, addicted to drinking and hunting more than farming. The old man breeds a good number of horses on the rich flats; but his eldest daughter made a bad match of it, having married one Jackson, a notorious horse lifter, who was shot three years ago by the men of Maryland; and since that the old man has got into a pretty fix; he has to pay penalties of nearly £1,000, and besides, he has not paid the £1,000 due for the purchase of the meadows he holds; the interest of which he is even unable to pay. Now, you see, Sir Richard, I am employed by the owner of the land, and he has ordered me to sue for the penalties, and the fact is he will be turned out neck and crop, unless £2,000 be forthcoming before the end of September."

The Baronet listened attentively and eagerly; he felt assured that all the papers he possessed were forgeries, except the marriage certificate, and that, in fact, his first wife died in childbirth, and that by some means they had contrived to deceive Jay Pearson.

"Pray, Mr. Bowen," said the Baronet, "did you ever hear of a person called John Jay Pearson?"

"Yes, Sir Richard, I have; there was a person of that name came here some two or three years back in great distress and miserably ill; he, too, was enquiring for the Mason family, and John Mason assisted him; but who, or what he was, I cannot say. He died here shortly after his arrival."

The Baronet remained thoughtful for a minute, and then said: "Now, Mr. Bowen, if you can spare one day so as to give me your undivided attention and advice, I will become your debtor for fifty-pounds for that day, and any further business that may consequently arise shall be liberally settled for."

"You are very kind, Sir Richard," returned the Solicitor; "I can only say that I will be at your service whenever you wish, and with great pleasure assist you to the utmost of my ability in unraveling any intricate matter that requires one experienced in the law to elucidate."

"Then I will make you acquainted with every particular," said the Baronet, and he did so, and Mr. Bowen became perfectly well informed upon the subject of Sir Richard's first and second marriage. He also placed in the attorney's hands several papers, amongst them, Jay Pearson's confession.

Mr. Bowen read the latter document carefully. When finished he looked up into Sir Richard's face, saying: "This confession, Sir Richard, though exceeding well got up, is, in my opinion, all false; nevertheless, exceedingly likely to deceive you; my opinion is, that Jay Pearson himself was also deceived. May I ask you if John Mason's daughter was any way like Miss Grace Manning."

"Yes," returned the Baronet, thoughtfully, "remarkably alike when not seen together."

"Ah!" returned Mr. Bowen, "I think I see how Jay Pearson came to be deceived, especially in his then weak state, so near death, when he could scarcely be able distinctly to remark the features of the female introduced to him. As to the signatures they may be those of any rascals John Mason could pick up for a quart of whiskey. It can be easily proved that John Mason's daughter married Joe Jackson, who, as I told you, was shot, and the widow is at present with her father at Fork Farm. They are a bad lot, Sir Richard, but their machinations against you, though artfully contrived, are utterly worthless."

"Well, Mr. Bowen, I am of the same opinion as yourself; still, I must have full confirmation, and not only that, but I must have it from John Mason's own hand, that the whole is a deception. Miss Manning, my first wife, was a most amiable girl. Her son, of course, becomes my son and heir—Lady Morton is quite reconciled to that. The terrible blow we both apprehended, and which would have broken our peace of mind for ever in this world, once removed, we shall, indeed, gratefully acknowledge the goodness of Providence for the mercy we received. Will you, therefore, accompany me, to-morrow, to Fork Farm—and be a witness to my interview with John Mason?"

"Most certainly, Sir Richard, I will do so;

and take my chief clerk with us. There can be no deception practised now—you will see the daughter, said to be buried, instead of your first wife—and that alone will put an end to all doubt or uncertainty."

Sir Richard then arranged to start for Fork Farm at ten o'clock on the following morning, Mr. Bowen promising that his waggon, drawn by two stout horses, should be ready at that hour; so, shaking hands with the worthy attorney, Sir Richard returned to his inn, and sent for the farrier, who had so kindly offered him one of his horses to ride to the Fork. The man looked greatly surprised at his change of dress; but Sir Richard, giving him a couple of dollars, told him, he was going with a gentleman, on the morrow, in his waggon; but was equally obliged to him for his offer of a horse.

The next morning, a very light, handy, spring waggon, with a cover, and drawn by a pair of handsome iron grey horses, drew up to the inn door. Mr. Bowen was seated in it, with his clerk. The baronet soon joined them.

Two hours' drive over a very tolerable road, and through a well cultivated and picturesque country, brought them within sight of Fork Farm. It was so called from lying near a fork of the river. The house appeared a good substantial house of one story, and surrounded by several out buildings. The broad river ran within half a mile of the house. The land along the banks of the river was low and swampy; but by the house, and for a mile or two to the westward, it appeared a dead level, and nearly all pasture land. There was a bye road, more than a mile long, leading up to the house; this was in a wretched state of repair, and threatened every moment to smash the light waggon, being formed of trunks of trees, with great spaces between.

When within five hundred yards of the

farm yard they met two young men, with guns in their hands, and half a dozen fierce looking dogs coming towards them.

"Ah," said Mr. Bowen, "John Mason's two sons."

They came up to the waggon, keeping away the dogs, who seemed greatly inclined to attack the horses in the waggon.

"Holloa, neighbour!" said one of the young men, a strapping youth over six feet, and not more than twenty-two or twenty-three years of age. "I guess you're trying your springs rather hard. You had better walk to the house, if it's there you're going, for the next two hundred yards the timber is taken up; we're making a new road."

"And, I hope, a better one, Mr. William," said the Attorney, who had some misgiving about his springs.

Mr. William raised himself up on the shafts, and looked in.

"Ah," said he, in rather a surly tone, "it's you, Charles Bowen. I guess father don't require visits from chaps of your kidney. Who's the stranger with you?" and both young men, very unceremoniously, got up and sat on the side of the waggon, looking with a bold stare into Sir Richard's face.

"This gentleman is from England," said the Attorney, motioning with his hand to Sir Richard, who was looking earnestly into the faces of the two young men, of whom he had not the slightest recollection, for they were mere boys when their father left England.

"I guess my father don't want to see any gentleman from the old country. What's your business, stranger?" added the eldest of the two, looking the baronet fixedly in the face.

"That I shall tell John Mason when I see him," quietly replied Sir Richard, rising up, and turning to address the attorney:—

"Mr. Bowen, I think we may walk the rest of the way."

He was preparing to get out, when the young men said, with a laugh:—

"I calculate you had better not step down; those dogs of ours may like the least taste in the world of your hide—they ain't particular."

"Then, sir, get down and call them away," said the baronet, haughtily. "I must see your father."

"There's no must in the case," returned the young man named William, doggedly. "What's your name—I guess you've a name?"

"Come, this is trifling," said the baronet. "My name is Morton—Sir Richard Morton, of Morton Chase. You remember those names, young as you were when you left England. I cannot say that your manners are improved — your courtesy certainly not."

The two young men looked entirely confounded—staring with open mouth, and a bewildered look at the baronet, who was eyeing the six huge dogs sitting on their haunches, glaring up at the waggon, evidently eager for some pretence to commence hostilities.

Mr. Bowen looked rather startled. As to the clerk, there was no mistake in his appearance, for he never took his eyes off the dogs.

"You had better drive on, James," said Mr. Bowen to the driver; "the waggon will stand worse than this, I've tried it."

The two young men jumped down without a word and, calling the dogs, walked rapidly towards the house, with their guns on their shoulders.

"Drive on," said Sir Richard, eagerly, to the driver; "if we break down I will pay for a dozen waggons sooner than not get to the house as soon as those uncouth youngsters."

James gave the horses the reins, and a touch of the whip; away they went, bumping the waggon over the trunks of trees, and making the passengers stand up and grasp the sides; but, nevertheless, they entered the large farm yard at the same time as the two

Masons. Coming out from the house, hearing the noise and the barking of the dogs, an old man and two women were seen; the eldest of the two looked up surprised, at observing the waggon, and at the excited manner of the two young Masons, who called out:—

"Go in, d—— you—go in and shut the door!"

It was too late. Sir Richard, who was standing up in the front of the waggon, had fixed his eager glance on the women; the moment the elder female looked up, he called out:

"Thank God! there is Eliza Mason alive and well!" and at once jumped out; and, before any one could prevent him, or understand his motives, he caught the old man, standing at the door looking bewildered, by the arm, saying—

"John Mason, you cannot but remember me; I am Sir Richard Morton."

As he spoke, two of the fierce dogs, seeing him grasp their master, rushed furiously towards him, but the youngest daughter drove them off, the two younger Masons leaning on their guns, with a fierce, troubled expression on their countenances. Two or three farm men had also come out from a large barn.

John Mason, a strong man, still hale at sixty-five, trembled in every limb, as he heard Sir Richard declare his name; but he recollected him at the same moment. This fear only lasted a moment; the colour rushed back to his cheeks, and, releasing his arm, he stepped back, saying, in a firm voice, "Well, Sir Richard—suppose I am John Mason? I am in a free country, and have committed no crime against its laws."

The two females drew near their father, both gazing fixedly and most anxiously into Sir Richard's face.

"I do not accuse you, John Mason," said Sir Richard, calmly, "of anything of the kind; let us go in. I wish to do nothing against you, whatever, although," he added, lowering his voice, so that only John Mason heard his words, "Your son attempted to murder me, and left me for weeks, hovering between life and death."

John Mason staggered back, pale as death, saying, "And George—he is"—the rest of the words stuck in his throat.

"He has escaped as yet," returned the baronet, "but I know nothing of him; he stabbed me, and robbed me of five hundred pounds I intended for him,—but come in—I again say I mean you no harm." Then, turning to the eldest of the females, who looked very sullen, he said, "Come in with us, Mrs. Jackson, I am, you may well judge why, very happy to see you alive and well."

Mrs. Jackson's eyes flashed. She was still a very fine handsome woman of forty; but neither her manners nor her morals had improved, since her departure from England, and her marriage with a notorious horse-lifter. As she turned away, and joined her two brothers, she said, with intense bitterness, "You may live yet to regret that I am alive."

"I hope not, Mrs. Jackson," returned the baronet, calmly. "I mean you no ill, nor anyone present." He then walked into the house, followed by Mr. Bowen and his clerk; the latter would have given a week's salary to have been back again in Delawarr.

John Mason walked sullenly into a large room, evidently the great kitchen and sitting-room of the family.

"Well, Sir," said John Mason, as the baronet seated himself on a bench, "what do you expect to gain by this visit? You see that my daughter lives, and I suppose that satisfies your conscience."

"No," said the baronet, sadly; for as he looked into John Mason's features, the memory of the past came vividly before him, and, alas! the past had many cruel memories in it.

"I am, however," continued Sir Richard, "so far satisfied, for now I feel a great relief, being saved from committing a great wrong."

"Aigh, Aigh," fiercely broke in John

Mason. "No doubt; no doubt you thought in your youth nothing of destroying a poor orphan girl. Knowing that you had me in your power you artfully induced me to second your wicked designs. I pretended to aid you, but, nevertheless, I baffled you."

"Then, why, John Mason," sternly interrupted the baronet, "knowing that Grace Manning was truly my wife, did you not at once say so, and save me, twelve months after, from deserting my child?"

"I did not tell you," returned John Mason fiercely, "because Jay Pearson was as great a rascal as any in England. I took your child and put it where I knew it would be taken care of, whilst I continued my search and enquiries after Jay Pearson, who disappeared after what you supposed to be a mock ceremony. I afterwards informed your sister who the father of the child was. Had its mother lived, my plans would have been very different. But all this is useless talk. You have certainly defeated my son's project. But why he should attempt your life, is to me a mystery. What was it for?"

"Because," returned the baronet, "I attempted to take the papers he said he possessed, from him; and here they are," he continued, taking Jay Pearson's confession and others, from his vest. "In the struggle we had, he dropped them on the floor, then stabbed me, and also robbed me of the very five hundred pounds I had on my library table, and which were intended for him."

"Ah!" said the old man, bitterly, "he only stabbed you in self-defence. I know he never intended to hurt a hair of your head. You only reaped what you sowed."

"Come, John Mason," said Sir Richard, "cease this bitterness; let the past be, alas! not forgotten, but let it be looked upon with regret and repentance. My youth has been one of sin and sorrow. On a bed of suffering for weeks, I learned to look upon the errors of my youth with intense sorrow and regret, and vowed, if God spared me, to atone for the evil I had committed.

"I did not come here to reproach you, for we are equally guilty. I came to assure myself that I was spared the commission of a second crime, and that the remainder of my life might not be embittered by beholding the tears and the sorrows of an amiable woman and her innocent offspring. Thank God, from that I am spared; and now listen to me, John Mason,—it is in my power to make you some atonement for the past. You are in difficulties; you will lose your lands if you do not pay two thousand pounds before next September."

John Mason looked eagerly into Sir Richard Morton's features; as he ended, he said, "I am involved. I became liable to a thousand pounds penalty, from my son in law's acts; and the purchase-money for the best part of this farm is unpaid. We shall be driven out of house and land, if these debts remain unpaid in two months. I have no right to expect help from you, Sir Richard, that I well know."

"Never mind that now," said the baronet; "we have both erred," and taking out his pocket book, he took from it a blank cheque, upon a New York Bank; looking for pen and ink, he filled it up for three thousand pounds, saying, "I lodged this money in the Bank at New York. In case this important affair ended amicably, which I now hope it will, I forgive the past; do you the same, John Mason, and accept this, it will release you from your difficulties and leave you a thousand pounds for future use." And the baronet handed the cheque to the amazed and overpowered old man; for several moments he appeared unable to speak, his hand trembled as it held the paper, which he put at once into a pocket book, and the muscles of his face worked with some internal emotion he strove to conquer.

"But if my misguided son," said John Mason, "is taken—"

"I will not appear against him," said the baronet. "The accusation against him for making away with my son, which he did, according to my wishes, though he carried that project out quite contrary to my instructions, I can easily stop. My son is by this time in Jamaica. I shall write immediately for his return, and establish his rights. All I ask of you is to permit this gentleman, Mr. Bowen, who is acquainted with all the particulars, to draw up the necessary papers to establish his claims, and proofs of his birth and his mother's marriage and death; and should your son George escape out of England, which I expect he has by this time, that you will exert your influence and prevent his ever returning there."

John Mason, relieved from a state of destitution, for Mr. Bowen had told him that the entire family would be expelled the farm, felt eager to perform every wish of the baronet's, in fact he strove all in his power to shew that he could be grateful. He sent for his two sons, but they had left the farm, and so had Mrs. Jackson, and gone, the workmen said, in their light waggon to the Fork, where they had some store houses. However, Mr. Bowen and his clerk, delighted at the change of affairs, and being provided with materials, drew up every necessary paper to fulfil Sir Richard's wishes. These were only rough drafts. The old man engaged to come the next day to the attorney's office and sign the proper documents before responsible witnesses. The youngest daughter, Emily, a very pretty and interesting young woman, busied herself eagerly in putting the best refreshments the house afforded in a small parlour off the kitchen. The horses were taken out of the waggon and fed, and the utmost harmony apparently prevailed.

Sir Richard, whilst Mr. Bowen and his clerk were employed in the little parlor, had a long and serious conversation with his former steward. It appeared by this conversation that much of the plotting and scheming of the Mason family was concocted by the sons, George Mason especially.

The baronet having settled and arranged everything to his entire satisfaction, and Mr. Bowen having finished his labours, they prepared to return to Delawarr. John Mason appeared to have regained heart and spirits; the prospect of freeing his farm and himself from the clutches of his creditors, without further plotting or crime, seemed to give him new life.

Thus all parted, exceedingly well pleased the one with the other. The baronet released from a load of bitter reflections, and with a sincere feeling of repentance for his past errors, and firmly resolved to do his duty by his first-born, no matter how trying the ordeal, he would have to go through.

It was late that night when Sir Richard and his solicitor reached Delawarr; the next morning he moved with his luggage into the best hotel the town afforded.

CHAPTER IX.

John Mason was punctual to time and place, and faithfully performed his part of the contract. Mr. Bowen drew up all the necessary documents to substantiate the baronet's first marriage and the birth of his son, by his first wife, had them witnessed by three highly respectable citizens and a magistrate, and then John Mason, after taking leave of Sir Richard with a good deal of apparent emotion on his part, returned to his farm.

Three days more completed the baronet's business, and settling with Mr. Bowen in a most munificent manner, he set out for Williamsburg, on his return to Europe, a happier and better man than when he left its shores.

At this period there were no railroads from Delawarr to Williamsburg, only a kind of stage waggon that carried some fifteen or eighteen persons of all grades, seated promiscuously in this conveyance, which was covered with a canvas awning, and drawn by four active horses.

As Sir Richard had suffered considerably in this conveyance on reaching Delawarr, he resolved to travel as far as Williamsburg on a hired horse, with a guide also mounted, his luggage being forwarded by the waggon.

The country for miles after leaving the town of Delawarr was a most uninteresting flat, with here and there some very well cultivated lands. About eight miles from Delawarr the road takes a bend in the direction of Fork Farm, and enters a thick forest with a wide good road through it, formed of trunks of trees, covered with gravel. Sir Richard, as he rode along, became deeply immersed in thought; he heeded very little either the road, or the scenery around it. His guide, who was riding some fifty or sixty yards in advance, was suddenly startled by the sharp report of a rifle in his rear; turning round, to his horror and dismay, he beheld Sir Richard Morton fall senseless from his horse, and lie motionless upon the road. For a moment he was incapable of motion; when another report, and the whizzing of a ball close to his head, so startled the lad, that digging his spurs into his horse, he galloped without pulling in for two miles, and then stopped before a small public-house, where horse travellers often stopped to refresh their steeds.

The ill-fated Sir Richard Morton lay dead upon the road, on his back—the ball had pierced his heart.

No sooner had the guide disappeared than two men attired in wagoners' frocks, and leather leggings, their faces concealed in the folds of thick handkerchiefs, came hastily forth from the thick belt of trees, and after a keen scrutiny all round, they approached the dead body of the Baronet, and one kneeling down commenced searching all the pockets, but swearing a terrible oath he said to his companion:

"Baulked by ——, not a paper of any kind in his pockets."

"Curse it, then we have killed him for nothing. Let us go, we have had our revenge at all events."

The other ruffian stamped upon the ground in a savage passion, saying:

"I cannot understand it. What can he have done with them? He told Bowen, my father heard him say it, that no inducement would cause him to put them from his person till he reaches England, and I'm —— if there's a paper to be found."

"Then," as I said, "we have killed him for nothing."

"Curse it; this is a bad job," returned the other; "but take all the valuables and cash he has and let us be off; the waggon from Williamsburg will be here in an hour or so."

Having completely rifled the Baronet's pockets the two men retreated into the wood, took up their rifles from behind a tree, and walked at a rapid pace, for nearly a mile through the wood, till they came to a spot where two strong and handsome horses might be seen fastened by pegs to the ground. Without losing a moment, the two men mounted, and rode off at a rapid pace.

This cold blooded and brutal murder was committed in broad daylight, on the main road between Delawarr and Williamsburg. The two murderers rode across the country till they came to a road framed with timber, close beside a river; along this they continued, travelling very leisurely and conversing. These heartless villains were the sons of John Mason, of Fork Farm, and their vile and ungrateful father was an accomplice in the fearful act they had committed.

"There will no doubt be a rigid inquiry as

to who killed the Baronet," said Charles Mason to his brother William.

"Not a bit of it," returned the other, "and if there is, our plan is so well arranged that I defy detection; but curse it, where are the papers? What we have got is not worth fifty pounds; whereas, the papers would have been worth five thousand to that Arthur Bolton, who is the Baronet's real heir, for without them, he cannot claim either the estates or the title."

"It is a bad job, killing him," returned the other brother rather moodily. "Now there's nothing to be had for the job, I wish I had never listened to our sister's vindictive hatred of Sir Richard."

"To the devil with your qualms of conscience," returned the elder brother—the one who fired the shot. "He has only got what he richly deserved. Didn't he wrong our family in every way—didn't he try to deceive our sister and afterwards our cousin by a false marriage. He made father his tool, and intended to cast us all off, his rightful relations, with a pitiful present of £3000—that barely clears the Fork Farm of its incumbrances—and then there's our brother's life in jeopardy in England through him. Curse me, if I regret killing him; the loss of the papers maddens me. Confound his cunning, what could he have done with them; not surely sent them with his baggage to Williamsburg again. Why did he change his place of embarcation? Why did he not return to New York?"

"I should not wonder if that Welsh rascal Bowen put him up to some dodge about those papers. I should like to put a bullet through that Taffy's head," said the younger brother, savagely; "he holds the bonds against Fork Farm. First opportunity I get, he shall have one—but here's the ford—get down and unbridle our beasts and turn them across the river into Patten's farm, and we can come back for them in a day or two."

The two men alighted, took off the horses' bridles—saddles they had none—and putting the horses into the river, they drove them across into a range of low lying meadows, where numerous cattle were grazing. The whole of this tract of country was, at this period, very thinly inhabited, the farms few and far between. They were then only three miles from Fork Farm, but they remained under shelter of a thick wood, for it began to rain heavily, till quite dusk; they then crossed the country into their own land, and gained the house without being seen by any of the farm servants of the place, who always retired to rest with the cessation of daylight.

The old man and the eldest daughter, Mrs. Jackson, were the only persons up in the house. They were sitting in the great kitchen, the old man drinking repeated tumblers of strong whiskey toddy, the daughter helping herself to a share.

"They are very late," said the old man, who, notwithstanding his potations, looked very pale and agitated; he was not an habitual drinker, but this night he drank hard. "I wish we hadn't agreed to do this terrible deed."

And he trembled and rocked himself in his chair.

"Pshaw! you've grown a coward, father," said Mrs. Jackson, scornfully. "You forget our wrongs. I don't believe him, that my brother has escaped. Did he not," she savagely continued, "deceive me? he tried to make me his mistress till he saw Grace Manning, and then he scorned me. I don't forget—hark!"

And she paused.

As the father and daughter listened they heard a slight noise at the back of the house, and then a key turn softly in a lock.

"Ah!" she exclaimed, "they are come back."

And even she turned pale, but thoroughly contaminated by her marriage with a desperate horse stealer, she soon recovered herself, and proceeded to the back kitchen to open the inner door.

None of the male farm servants slept in the house, but were located in a large building at the further end of the farm yard. Two female servants, however, slept in the house with the family, in the east end. for it was a very long building.

Emily Mason, the youngest daughter, in every way totally different from the rest of the members of that terrible family, had retired, as was her custom, early to rest.

It will be here necessary to state that a farm adjoining the Fork farm, but separated by the river, was occupied by a man of the name of Patten. This man was a suitor for the hand of Emily Mason, but being of a somewhat doubtful character, Emily did not very much favour his suit; her brothers hated him, for it was owing to him that Mrs. Jackson's husband was detected in one of his horse lifting expeditions, and frequent fights and disputes took place between him and the brothers.

Luke Patten was to all appearance well to do in the world, and held a very large farm.

When Mason got into trouble, Patten resumed his offer of taking Emily for a wife, and besides offered to help her father in clearing the Fork farm. The old man was willing enough, and even partly succeeded in persuading Emily to listen to his proposals, when a violent dispute occurred between the brothers and Luke Patten, about a piece of land, and a fight took place, in which Luke Patten was the victor, and then a deadly hatred between the families took place, and all intercourse ceased. Such was the state of affairs at the time of Sir Richard Morton's visit to Fork farm.

Mrs. Jackson having admitted her brothers, they threw off their soaked over garments, and followed their sister in a very sulky, savage humour into the kitchen.

The old man looked up, saying, in a trembling voice—

"Have you the papers?"

"No; curse it," fiercely exclaimed William Mason, "we shot him dead; but he had no papers about his person."

"Good Heaven!" stammered out the old man, and his hands fell powerless upon the table. "Ah," he muttered, "another crime and no use. So he's dead?"

And he looked up into his eldest son's face, who was helping himself to a horn of whiskey in its pure state.

"Yes," he returned, putting down the horn, "dead enough."

"But how was it that you lost the papers —the papers were what you did this—this—"

"Murder, for," said the son, savagely, seeing his father pale and trembling.

"William, William, why do you use that word," said John Mason, shaking as if in an ague. "I am sure he had the papers concealed on his person. Did you search every part of his clothing?"

"I tried every pocket, and the linings in the breast of his coat, and his great coat, and took all he possessed, that it may be thought he was robbed for his cash and watch, for his is not the first robbery and murder that has been committed on that road."

"Did you try or feel the back of his coat," asked the old man, with a sudden start, and grasping William Mason by the arm, and gasping almost for breath.

"Feel the back of his coat," repeated the son, with a slight change of color, "what the deuce makes you think of that?"

"Then you did not?" said the old man, with a groan. "What a forgetful old fool I am. I now remember Sir Richard" (he shuddered, as he pronounced the name) "said 'he would have a double lining put to his coat, and the back was the best place as the papers would be flat.' Oh, fool! that I was not to recollect the observation."

William and Charles Mason looked at each other, uttering a savage oath at their own stupidity in not turning the body of the baronet round, for he lay on his back in the middle of the road, and they contented themselves with trying all the pockets and ripping open the lining of the breasts of the two coats. The back being an unusual repository, and the body pressed heavily on the garments, they observed nothing to attract their attention.

"Well, there's no use cursing and fretting about the matter," said Mrs. Jackson, "he's justly punished for the way he treated our family. We have the £3,000 to clear the farm, and that's something."

"Give me the pocket book out of the desk," said the old man, trembling, and his voice hoarse, and his lips blanched, though he swallowed a full horn of whiskey toddy at a draught.

"What do you want with the pocket book?" said Mrs. Jackson, with a sneer. "You are weaker than a child, and look as if the ghost of your old accomplice was standing up before you."

"Do see if the cheque is all right, we were

all so confused and scared by his coming so suddenly upon us, that I took the cheque after he drew it without looking at it."

"Pooh!" interrupted the son, as Mrs. Jackson opened a massive oak chest in a corner of the room, "it's all right you may be sure, and for fear of accident, I'll cash it to-morrow at the Branch Bank in Delawarr."

Mrs. Jackson took out the pocket book and gave it to her father. He put on his spectacles, and with trembling hands unclosed the book and fumbled through some papers till he came to the cheque. One look and with a groan of agony he tossed his arms up and then his head fell heavily upon the table.

The son seized the cheque, and gazing at it, with a fearful oath, struck the table violently, saying: "By —— he neglected to sign it, it is worthless."

The old man never stirred. Mrs. Jackson, aghast, and now trembling herself, raised her father's head, and then with a piercing shriek, let it fall back on the table, and then sunk fainting in a chair. John Mason was dead.

Before night came, the inhabitants of Delawarr were roused into a state of uncommon excitement. The dead body of the unfortunate Sir Richard Morton was brought into the town by the stage waggon from Williamsburg, and deposited in a chamber of the same hotel he had left in the morning in health and spirits. Mr. Bowen, who was known to be the confidential adviser of the deceased baronet, was sent for.

The consternation of the worthy attorney was overpowering; for some moments he remained overwhelmed with grief and dismay. Then he thought of the valuable papers—papers of such consequence to the baronet's heir, that he seized his hat and rushed late as it was to the hotel.

In the parlour he found Mr. Baxter and Mr. Fowler, the two chief magistrates in the town.

"This is a horrible affair, Mr. Bowen,"

said Mr. Baxter, "an English gentleman of rank murdered and robbed within twelve miles of the town; there has not been an act of the kind committed since Mr. George Carver was shot down and robbed, by two of his own tenants, and that's nearly two years ago. You were intimately acquainted with the gentleman during his short stay here, Mr. Bowen. Have you any reason to suspect anyone?"

"Has Sir Richard Morton's coat been searched?" demanded the attorney, most anxiously.

"His pockets were cleared out, I can tell you," said Mr. Fowler, "and the lining of his coat on the front had been ripped open."

"But was the back of his coat searched?" questioned Mr. Bowen, "for I know he had a case of soft leather made to contain sheets of paper of great—of vast importance. In fact, Mr. Fowler, you yourself witnessed the signing of those papers by old John Mason, of Fork Farm—your name and two respectable citizens besides are attached to them."

"Let us proceed instantly and have the coat searched," said Mr. Fowler, "the body lies on its back, and no one has touched the coat or taken off any of the garments."

All three, attended by the landlord with lights, proceeded to the chamber where the body lay covered with a cloth.

Mr. Bowen shuddered as the landlord threw back the sheet and disclosed the face of the deceased baronet.

The handsome features of Sir Richard Morton still retained their beauty; there was a placid calm repose in the noble features, but little altered by the hand of the destroyer. Death, by a gun-shot wound, leaves no traces of agony in the features of the dead.

"He was a very handsome man," said Mr. Baxter, "and still in his prime—not fifty I should say."

"No, not fifty," said the attorney, much affected. "Alas! what an ill-timed choice it was of his to ride to Williamsburg, and not travel in the stage waggon."

"We must have a searching inquiry into this brutal murder and robbery, Mr. Bowen, to-morrow. Just put your hand along the back of the coat, and see if the papers you speak of are there. They would be of no use to a robber."

The landlord raised the body, and Mr. Bowen searched the coat.

"Good God! they are gone," he exclaimed, turning very pale; "the lining is cut entirely away."

"Then this murder has been committed for the sake of those papers. I will have the whole family at Fork Farm arrested the first thing in the morning," said Mr. Bowen vehemently. "No human being could have had the slightest interest in those papers, except the Masons."

"Ah," said the magistrates, "they're a bad lot; the two sons and that fellow Jackson, the horse lifter, were notorious at one time. They shall be arrested—father and sons, the first thing in the morning," said both magistrates. As they all retired from the room, Mr. Bowen shook Mr. Baxter and Mr. Fowler by the hand, saying, "I will defray all expenses incurred by the funeral, and will communicate at once with the family of Sir Richard Morton."

The following morning six armed constables with an officer of police proceeded to Fork Farm to arrest John Mason and his two sons.

They were seen approaching the house and Mrs. Jackson felt overpowered. William and Charles Mason, who had made up their minds how to act, betrayed no fear. They considered their plans so well laid as to be impossible of detection, so desiring Mrs. Jackson to go up to her sister, who was fearfully grieved at the death of their father, very coolly opened the door to the police officer and the constables.

"Well, mister," said William Mason, in a contemptuous tone, "are you come to turn us out of the farm, if you are, you're a day too late."

"I am come, Mr. Mason," said the police officer, "to arrest you, your brother, and your father on suspicion of being concerned in the murder and robbery of Sir Richard Morton."

"You don't say that the baronet has been murdered!" said both brothers, with a well-feigned start, and then with an oath, "if so, we are ruined."

"Where is your father," said the officer, a little surprised.

William Mason threw open the door of the kitchen and walked in; the officer and constables followed, when William Mason threw off a cloth from a table, all started back, for laid out on it was the body of John Mason.

"How is this?" exclaimed the officer. "When did he die, and what the cause of death?"

"He died suddenly last night, when sitting at table; all the family were present except my youngest sister. He has for some time suffered from disease of the heart."

"Have you sent for any doctor, or have you let the coroner know?" asked the officer, "this is a sudden death."

"We have sent to both those functionaries," said the son. "I expect them every moment. You have accused us of a crime—"

"Which I saw you commit with my own eyes, William Mason," exclaimed a loud, bold voice, and then a tall, powerful young man, carrying a rifle in his hand, and who pushed through the surprised constables and entered the room, stood facing William and Charles Mason with an expression of stern, implacable hate.

The brothers fell back, pale as death, exclaiming: "Patten—Luke Patten," and then in a burst of passion William Mason started up, and with a face purple with rage, shouted "Liar! you are stating this lie from malice and a desire to destroy us."

"If you had been destroyed years ago,"

fiercely interrupted Luke Patten, "it would have been better for you than to die now steeped in crime."

What followed was the work of scarcely a minute. Both brothers were powerful, active men; with a sudden and irresistible bound they sprang amidst the constables, dashing three to the ground, and gained the door. Luke Patten never stirred to prevent them. The constables and the police officer, furious with rage, rushed after them, but the fugitives had banged to the heavy massive door of the farm house, and several minutes elapsed before they could open it. When they did, they saw several farm men standing in the yard, looking stupified and bewildered, but the brothers were nowhere to be seen. There was a thick cover at the back of the farm, and through this they had rushed. Four of the constables hotly pursued, but the brothers had snatched up two bridles off a hook, ran into the far Paddock, and at once caught two strong young horses, and before the constables could come up, had mounted and galloped off at a furious pace, escaping the pistol shots fired at them.

The noise, confusion, flight, and pursuit, had alarmed the two sisters above. Mrs. Jackson had recovered her nerve and resolution. Emily, who knew nothing of the plot between the rest of her family, to destroy Sir Richard Morton, was terribly afflicted by the sudden death of her father. Mrs. Jackson ran up-stairs, on seeing the constables. Pale and startled, Emily said, "What is the matter, Eliza—you look so fearfully pale; who are those men whose voices I hear?"

"They are constables, and a police-officer," said Mrs. Jackson—sinking into a chair.

"What can they want?" said Emily, surprised. "Such men can have no business here. Sir Richard Morton's generosity has freed us from all fear of being turned out of the farm."

"They are not here for that," returned Mrs. Jackson, sharply. "You were always different from the rest of us—not a bit like one of us. Talk of Sir Richard's generosity, indeed, after destroying our family, and, for recompence, giving our father an unsigned cheque for three thousand pounds."

"Hark! I hear Luke Patten's voice," said Emily, starting up, and turning pale—for it was now nearly sixteen months since a complete rupture between the two families had taken place. As the two women stood listening, they heard their brothers rush out, and slam the house door, and, going to the windows, they beheld them clear the farm-yard wall, and then saw the constables in pursuit.

"Good God!" cried Emily, "what is all this about? Why do our brothers fly; and why do those men pursue them?"

Mrs. Jackson made no reply, but ran down stairs, and Emily Mason, her heart beating painfully, followed.

In the kitchen, the police-officer and Luke Patten were standing, earnestly conversing.

For a moment Mrs. Jackson hesitated, whilst Emily trembled, without the power to move. Patten advanced towards Emily, and said, in a low tone, "This is a terrible affair, Miss Emily, and I regret that a sense of justice forces me to become the accuser of your two brothers, having seen them commit a fearful crime."

"You—you—Luke Patten," exclaimed Mrs. Jackson, in a tone of intense passion, and pushing her trembling and half-fainting sister aside, "and do you dare to come under this roof to gratify your hatred by uttering a monstrous lie?"

"Why did your brothers fly, then, if they were innocent," said Luke Patten, calmly.

"Well, this is quite a useless argument, now," interrupted the police-officer, "and I have no time to waste. Mr. Mason is dead, and his two sons have escaped for the present, but they will be caught; and you, Mr. Luke Patten, must be ready when called upon, to give evidence as an eye witness of this atrocious murder."

"Merciful God! what murder—who is murdered!" said Emily Mason, staggering up to Joseph Patten, catching him by the arm, and looking him anxiously in his face.

"I grieve, Miss Emily, to say," said the young man, "that Sir Richard Morton, an English gentleman, was cruelly murdered, and by your brothers William and Charles."

Emily uttered a wild cry of anguish, and would have fallen on her face, but Luke Patten caught her in his arms, and placed her in a chair in the kitchen, leaving her to the care of the two terrified female attendants of the family.

In this state, we must leave not only the vicinity of Fork farm, but the shores of the North American continent, and return to the waters of the Punza Pulka river, where we left our hero.

CHAPTER X.

WE left Arthur Bolton and his faithful and attached follower, Joseph, proceeding up the Punza Pulka river in the small dingy belonging to the cutter, to shoot a few duck and teal for the use of the cabin of the Foam. In fact Arthur thought he would have more leisure for thought during his excursion, upon his approaching meeting with Alice Marchmont's father. He felt much uneasiness at this meeting, knowing how utterly without name, fortune, or friends, he stood in the world. It appeared to him, therefore, notwithstanding Mrs. Marchmont's sanguine view of his wishes and their realization, a very doubtful affair, particularly with a man of Mr. Marchmont's character and disposition.

Joe, who was looking out for game, and had nothing to think of particularly, was steering the boat as she ran up the river with a strong tide, called the attention of our hero to a large flock of the white ibis:

"Are they fit to eat, sir?" asked Joe, "faix they are as big as a goose."

"But not half as good, Joe; there's a large flight of teal over on the east shore, they are on the wing at present, but they will soon light. A good shot with my double-barrel will bag a supply for two or three days. Edge the boat on, Joe."

Joe did so, but the teal took a sudden whirl and went much further up the river. Our hero could have killed several single birds, ducks and teal, but he preferred keeping his shot for the great flock.

"There will be a storm, Joe," said Arthur Bolton, "or some great change in the weather, the flocks are so exceedingly uneasy."

Just however as they came near the opening of the creek that led into the Tonza Lagoon, he had a famous double shot into a large flock sailing out of the creek. Seventeen teal was the result, after a long chase up the creek after the wounded.

"Come, this will do," said our hero. "A few more ducks now will furnish our larder well."

"Look, sir," said Joe, "there are a dozen macaws and parrots chattering, with their young ones on the ground. I could catch one or two easily."

"Let us try," said our hero, without thinking of his promise to Alice not to land, "but let us be quick, for the tide is on the turn."

Fastening the boat, they proceeded in search of the macaws.

Arthur Bolton had not the most remote idea, that from the moment he approached the entrance of the creek he was most keenly watched from the shore by a party of men, with the most deadly intentions, creeping amongst the entangled mass of vegetation, which hid them completely from observation.

"Oh," said William Saunders, who was the leader of the party, who had been previously watching the movements of those aboard the brig and schooner, and whose intention was to board the little turtle schooner that our hero had possessed himself of, when he carried off Alice, and endeavour to get her to sea.

"Oh," said William Saunders, with a ferocious oath—"If I could only get him within sure shot."

The villain had his face bound by a band passing round his head, for the shot fired by Arthur Bolton on the night he rescued Alice had broken his jaw, and fearfully disfigured him. He was willing to sacrifice life if he could only be sure of killing Arthur Bolton.

"Maladetta!" returned one of the Mexicans. "Have patience, they will surely land; see, they are coming into the creek."

"Ah, curse him! I'll not shoot him, I'll give him days of torture before I finish him. Keep cautiously out of sight, do not tread even on a twig."

Thus watching, and getting within pistol shot, the four men saw those in the dingy land. Arthur Bolton was standing under a magnificent cotton-tree, close to the bank of the creek, and Joe had just failed in catching a young macaw, when our hero received a heavy blow from the butt of a musket, from behind, which felled him, bewildered, and for the moment senseless, at the feet of Saunders. Joe had turned round, perceived the fate of his master, and just as two of the Mexicans rushed at him to seize him, he fired his gun full in the face of the foremost, killing him on the spot, and then, dropping his gun, plunged into the creek and dived, thus escaping the shots fired at him by the furious Mexicans.

Before they could again load, Joe had gained the other shore, and rushed into the dense jungle on that side.

The frantic maledictions and oaths of the ruffians thus baffled, were horrible to hear. As to Saunders, he cared nothing about the dead Mexican, he stood exultingly with his foot upon the body of his victim, uttering the most savage threats. He had bound Arthur's hands and legs securely, before he had time to recover from the effects of the blow, and stood glaring at his victim as a tiger would his prey, before he tore him to pieces. Arthur Bolton had become quite conscious, and his first look into the face of his unrelenting enemy, told him mercy for him was not to be.

"What's to be done," asked one of the Mexicans, sulkily, if not savagely, glaring at Saundērs, whom they all detested, but who had, in their then desperate state, gained a temporary mastery over them. "That infernal youth has killed Carlo."

"More fool Carlo, to let himself be killed by such an urchin. Why didn't you shoot him? we didn't want him alive. Go and send the punt adrift, upset it, and let it go down with the tide. Those aboard the brig will think them drowned."

"What shall we do with the body of our comrade?" grumbled the others.

"Do with it," said Saunders with an oath, for every word he uttered gave him intense pain from his unhealed jaw. "You can't eat it, can you? Tie a heavy stone to it, and sink it in the creek."

The men growled and swore; but they proceeded to do Saunders's bidding.

"So," said that ruffian, as he saw Arthur Bolton make a desperate effort to free his hands; "you are in my power, at last. Curse you, what I have suffered through you," and taking a pistol from his belt, he pressed the muzzle against our hero's face. Stop your struggles—I could blow your infernal brains out now; but that would be a poor revenge for all that I have suffered from your —— interference."

"Villain! your own evil passions and vile nature have caused your sufferings."

"You lie!" roared the ruffian, and with a brutal cowardice he struck his helpless captive a blow across the mouth, that caused the blood to flow copiously.

Arthur Bolton felt choking with the internal emotion he experienced. He was resigned to die, but he saw that he was reserved for some terrible torture, and dark despair took possession of his soul, when the last words he heard his own Alice say occurred even in that dark moment to his memory:

"Even when hope is hopeless, there is still a hand to save; remember Captain Courtney!"

After a time the Mexicans returned, having sent the dingy adrift, and sunk the body of their comrade, Carlo. Then Saunders, putting additional cords on the wrists of his captive, cut those which bound his legs, and with an oath and a savage kick, cried:

"Get up, if you don't want me to slice you with my knife."

Praying to God to grant him patience and resignation, Arthur Bolton stood up, his dress was covered with blood, from the blow he had received in the mouth, and smarting pain in the head, from the deep gash made by the brass butted musket.

"What are you going to do with your prisoner?" asked the Mexican, who spoke English.

"Put him in the pit," said Saunders, "and let him die by inches. Pity that he will only take eight or ten days to die of starvation."

"We shall not get into the Lagoon to-night, there's a hurricane coming," said one Mexican.

"Then the sooner we launch the canoe the better," said Saunders; "the party in search of the girl, are no doubt aboard the brig by this time. That infernal rascal Punka Bosswash shall be served out yet before we quit the country."

Driving Arthur Bolton on before them, a strong breeze roaring through the thick wood, they reached the spot where they had left their canoe.

The three Mexicans, by no means satisfied, and grumbling and swearing at the loss of their comrade Carlo, launched the canoe, and then, as a precaution against any effort of their prisoner to escape, knowing his strength and daring, they firmly bound his legs together, thereby frustrating the very thing our hero intended to do—kick out the side of the canoe, and swamp her.

They lifted him in, and all entering, they paddled across the creek up to the weather side till they came to the rapids, where they landed, and lifted our hero out and hauled up the canoe. Saunders then freed his legs, and striking him brutally, forced him on before them, till they entered the same cave where our hero and Joe passed the night of the storm.

The Mexicans and Saunders were evidently

not on good terms—they did not like his plans, and they said so—but they feared him, and he cursed them bitterly.

On entering the cavern the prisoner perceived, that it had served for a habitation for those miscreants for several days; most likely they had taken refuge there to avoid the armed party of Mr. Marchmont when traversing the country in search of his daughter.

There were piles of wood heaped up, and the remains of a fire and pieces of the manitou hanging up.

Though it was very evident that the Mexicans hated Saunders, they nevertheless all shewed their vindictiveness to Arthur Bolton. One ruffian proposed to burn him alive. Saunders, ferociously assented; but immediately after said:

"No! death in the pit will be ten times worse."

"Well then, lower him down at once," said the Mexican, who spoke English—saying something to his comrades in a low voice. Yellow pine torches were then lighted.

During this time the captive had struggled hard, but in vain, to free his hands. He saw the Mexican knife in Saunders belt, and thought if he could have freed his hands and seized it, he would have fought desperately to avoid the horrible doom these wretches intended him; but he knew of no pit in the cave, and he gazed all round the cavern.

To define or analyse his thoughts during this painful moment would be scarcely possible—hope from human hands he had none—though he rejoiced at the escape of Joseph, still he knew he could get him no help, for the poor lad would be lost for hours in the wild jungle he had plunged into, and perhaps perish in it; his only chance of escape would be to swim the creek, and then endeavour to push his way along shore till opposite the vessels at anchor, and try and attract their attention.

Saunders and his comrades having fastened two cords together, seized Arthur Bolton in their grasp, and fastened the cord round his waist; whilst one carried a torch, the other three dragged him through the cavern till they came to a second cavern, in the middle of which was a yawning gulf. Arthur Bolton could not avoid shuddering. Saunders saw that he trembled.

"Ah," said he, with a ferocious laugh, the pain of which caused him to swear fearfully. "That's a nice place, seventy feet deep, and perpendicular. How long do you think you can live down there, eh? there's not much water down there now, but enough to cool your hot temper."

"Miserable wretch," said our hero, calmly, mastering every sign of fear or of emotion by a great effort. "There is an Almighty eye fixed upon you, even now. You think you triumph, but your brutal ferocious triumph will be short lived."

"Curse ye; do you think so," said Saunders. "No matter, you won't witness my doom whatever it will be—and now—off with him;" and he and his comrades gave a violent jerk to the rope, and Arthur swung helpless over the awful pit, down whose depths the light of the single torch threw but a very feeble gleam, revealing that its sides were almost perpendicular, and ascent from its depths impossible. With a horrible laugh, Saunders and his comrade held him swinging over the mouth, jerking him, and pretending to let him go.

Our hero suspecting what would be his fate, recommended his soul to his Maker, and murmuring the name of Alice, he closed his eyes. He heard the withering curse of the ruffian that he might live a week and suffer every pang hunger could inflict, and then he felt himself lowered, and roughly knocked against projecting rocks. Down he glided into the damp and suffocating hole, bruised and shaken, till suddenly the rope was let go, and he fell some feet, but he fell upright, and sank back in a cavity; for having his hands bound he had no power of resistance.

Scarcely had he fallen when a fearful yell rung through the place, and immediately came a strange sound, a kind of crash as of a body striking against the sides. Instinctively he drew his body nearer the fissure of the rocks, and the next moment, with a horrible squash, something fell with terrible violence at his feet. Then a dead silence prevailed. Our hero felt an indescribable horror, he could not breathe; he was sick at heart; and for the first time in his life his stout frame shook with a tremor like an ague. He was conscious that a body had been hurled into the pit, and had he not fallen into the cavity where he stood, he would have been crushed by the miserable wretch, whom instinct told him was William Saunders. Conquering the terrible emotions he felt, and recovering his nerve, he listened—was the man dead; but the next instant, a low, scarcely audible groan issued from the bruised mass at his feet. The man, whoever he was, was not dead, still he could not bring himself to move from where he was. Not a ray of light pierced the horrible darkness of the pit, for besides its depth, it was in a cavern where little or no light penetrated even in the broad day.

Did hope enter his breast, for suddenly Arthur Bolton recollected that if it was Saunders lying there he might still have his knife in his belt. Heavy groans came from the body and our hero thought words were spoken, and kneeling down, he turned his back and groped about the body; he felt the mass heave under his touch, and as he groped, a voice said: "I'm not dead—no—I'm not dead—curse you! I will live—live to hear you groan in your torture and despair." These words were spoken at intervals, as if the speaker was in horrible torture.

Doubtless every bone was broken, yet the wretched miscreant lived. Presently our hero's hand touched the knife, and he contrived to draw it from its sheath,—as he did so, he felt the grasp of a hand upon his arm; it was like a child's grasp, so feeble and impotent, but it showed that the mutilated wretch had still the power to move one arm.

"Do you want to murder me," gasped Saunders. "You can't escape—my cursed comrades pushed me over,"—and then followed a string of impotent curses and awful groans, as the mass of mangled bruized flesh strove to turn but uselessly, for the power to do so was gone for ever.

"Wretched man," said Arthur, "make your peace with God whilst you have still life, and a perception of your terrible, awful situation. I told you the hand of God was everywhere—His power infinite. I feel I shall yet escape from this horrid pit."

"Never!" shrieked the miserable wretch. "Never!—no one ever comes here—no—never,—I shall live as long as you—curse you—if you knew how I hate you."

"Yes," said Arthur Bolton, bitterly, "I think I ought to know, miserable man,—what did I ever do to cause this hate?"

For several minutes Saunders could not speak, from passion and agony. Strange to say, though a mangled mass, no vital part was touched. His legs and one arm were broken, his body bruised and mangled, but life still was strong within him, and those few hours of life were passed in uttering fearful oaths and imprecations. In the meantime, our hero had fixed the handle of the knife in a fissure of the rock, and then pressed and sawed the cords that bound his hands against its sharp edge, though he cut himself several times, still he freed his wrist, and then thanked God even for that relief.

Still there appeared no hope. By feeling the sides, he soon ascertained that the pit he was in was a deep rent in a mass of rocks, the sides being perpendicular as far as he could feel, the bottom was of small extent, and he judged from the ripling of water down the side, that in rainy seasons, a torrent ran down the cleft. After a time Saunders seemed to gain strength, as far as speaking went, for he kept venting imprecations and fearful denunciations against our hero.

"Don't think to escape. No, no. I'm sure of that; our bones will rot together."

At times he seemed to rave—he uttered such strange threats, and boasted of such horrid crimes.

"Do you know who you are?" he almost shrieked out, after a few minutes' silence. "It will make you more miserable, to know what a fine title and estate you might have had if I had not put you into this place."

"Miserable man, cease," said our hero, whose own thoughts were terrible enough, though he prayed to God, to give him patience and resignation. "You cannot have long to live."

"It's false!" interrupted Saunders; "you lie; I'll live to hear you curse your existence. Perhaps you'll eat me to prolong your life. Ha, ha!—eat me—that's good!"

"So you won't believe you're a great

man," again began Saunders, "when I tell you, Sir Richard Morton is your father—your lawful father. You're not a bastard."

Our hero started; even in his terrible position, the words uttered by the miserable Saunders, attracted his attention.

"Do you hear me? Curse you, do you hear me?" muttered Saunders, groaning with the intense agony he suffered as he strove to move his broken limbs; when he spoke there were at times long pauses between the words.

"Do you remember," he again began, after an interval, "the perfumer as he called himself—George Reynolds, his name was Mason; do you remember his companion, the sailor, who put you aboard the Foam; aigh, aigh! I know you do, though you won't speak. You are kneeling down close to me, I feel your breath. You're anxious; and a horrible death before you. I'll tell you all, for you will be the more miserable; you will never get out of this place. My bitter curses on those Mexican rascals." He paused, exhausted.

Arthur Bolton did feel a pang as he listened to the dying man's words—dying he was, and that rapidly, for the tones of his voice got weaker.

"Are you listening?" he began again, and he muttered something, and then commenced a rambling account of his own crimes, and after a time returned to his original subject. "Do you know that sailor was my brother, he, who helped Reynolds—Mason, I mean, to entrap you. I knew all about it. My brother told me if I had an opportunity to knock you on the head. I would have done so at the time of the mutiny, but for that meddling fool—the first mate—curse you, go out of that; what brings you here; don't you see Jackson, and our old captain standing grinning at me, and his little miserable steward hiding behind him. Oh, you don't frighten me; grin away; oh, gone, are you; don't come back;

you'll get nothing out of me." He then uttered a shriek of pain, and became still.

Arthur Bolton was horrified; we only repeat part of the wretched man's ravings. Sometimes they were too horrible to listen to. Our hero thought he was dead. He knelt beside him and listened. He could not hear him breathe, but finding his hand, he felt that his pulse beat weakly. The silence and dense darkness was horrible, and our hero prayed that his brain might not become affected. For nearly two hours, as well as he could judge, William Saunders lay breathing as light as an infant—not a word escaping his lips. Our hero placed his hand upon his face, the perspiration poured down his wasted features. "What sufferings this man is enduring," he uttered aloud. "Oh God, have pity and mercy upon him," and he felt the tears stealing down his own cheeks; suddenly he started, for a low, quiet voice said—

"Mr. Bolton, kneel close to me; I'm dying—quick, my time is short. You will be saved. I saw you saved in my dream. I heard you say you pitied me, and you even prayed to God to forgive me. I can't be forgiven—no, no—impossible!"

"Yes, yes," said Arthur Bolton. "Yes, God's mercy is infinite. You repent."

"I have dreamed," said Saunders, speaking low but distinctly, "you were saved. Hear me, put your hand on mine."

Our hero did so; it was wet as if it had been dipped in water.

"You thought," continued Saunders, "I was mocking you, when I said you were Sir Richard Morton's lawful son, but you are. Your mother was an orphan girl of good family. Grace Manning was her name—she died." He paused; and when he again spoke said—"moisten my lips with water. I hear it running down the rock." Our hero took some in the palm of his hand and passed it over the dying man's lips. He then said, "Your mother died in giving you life. Your father, the baronet, thought you were not his lawful son, for he believed the marriage ceremony between him and your mother was a sham, but it wasn't—a real clergyman married them. John Mason and his son George planned it all; hold my hand and pray for me, and oh, God, merciful God, forgive me!"

A violent shudder and a dreadful struggle took place. Our hero felt his hand grasped with wonderful fervour; the next moment William Saunders ceased to exist.

CHAPTER XI.

When Joe beheld Arthur Bolton stretched at the feet of Saunders, he thought him killed, and having shot the Mexican who endeavoured to seize him, he escaped by swimming the creek, and plunging into the dense jungle on the other side. After pushing his way into a tangled mass of vegetation, the poor lad paused and burst into a flood of tears. The supposed death of Arthur Bolton, to whom he had become devotedly attached, made him miserable. He listened for several moments to every noise, but the rising gale drowned every sound, as it raged amongst the trees and branches above him. "They have not pursued me,'' thought Joe. "Perhaps my master was only stunned. I will go back to see what they do with him. Retracing his way, he kept as close to the brink of the creek as he could with safety, keeping himself concealed under a mass of tangled vegetation, from whence, though concealed himself, he could distinctly see what passed on the opposite bank. The two Mexicans were just at that time turning over the dingy, and letting her go adrift into the Punza Pulka river.

"Ah, you cursed villains, I see you want to make believe we are drowned," muttered Joe. Seeing the two desperadoes returning upon the bank he continued to creep along his side also of the creek, and then to his intense delight he beheld his master, as he called him, alive, with his hands bound behind his back. He watched their proceedings with intense interest, and saw them put his master into the canoe, and then pull up towards the rapids. Determined to track them as far as he could, he continued cautiously to push his way through the jungle, now and then catching sight of the canoe, till they landed near the cave, and into which they went, driving Arthur Bolton before them. By this time it was nearly sunset. Another time Joseph would have felt intense horror at passing the night in the wild jungle without any weapon of defence, exposed to the attacks of wild beasts; but so intensely anxious was he about our hero's fate, that he forgot self entirely. He lay, therefore, stretched out, dripping wet as he was, in a mass of shrubs, not more than thirty or forty yards from the mouth of the cave, which he at once recognised as the same cavern where he and Arthur Bolton passed the night of the great flood and storm. As he lay straining his eyes, and eagerly watching the men, he felt the grasp of something upon his shoulder. Horror and fear prevented him uttering a cry, for a moment he could not even turn his head; he thought he was grasped by a wild beast, and every saint in his calendar was evoked to save him. The pressure was removed, and raising his head his eyes encountered, not a wild beast, but the dark, brilliant eyes of Achupa, the Indian girl.

Greatly amazed, he murmured, "Achupa." The Indian maid nodded her head and put her finger to her lips. She was lying at full length close behind him, and yet he had not heard the slightest noise—not even the snapping of a twig. It was very evident that the Indian girl knew what he was watching, for she resumed her gaze upon the mouth of the cave. Joe looked at the handsome Indian maid with wonder; her fine moulded limbs were as motionless as those of the dead; no part of her body stirred; she scarcely even breathed, so intense was her anxiety. Joe lay quiet, but it was not like the graceful statue-like composure of the child of the forest. She had a sharp iron-headed spear by her side, and at her back was her bow and quiver.

The gale howled through the jungle, and

the affrighted birds and animals uttered wild cries and sought shelter for the night. Soon the darkness of night spread over the forest, but the fires in the cave threw out a bright glaze. Presently the cry that Saunders uttered, when dashed into the pit by his treacherous comrades, startled the Indian girl and Joe. She sprang to her feet and drew her bow to the front. Joe was horror struck. Could the cry come from his master. A moment of thought satisfied him. No; such a cry as they heard, Arthur Bolton would never have uttered under any circumstances. Presently they beheld the three Mexicans come to the front of the cave, and throw some wood on the fire. The Indian girl laid her hand on Joe's, and counted three of his fingers. Saunders and our hero were missing. Joe would have given all he ever possessed if he could only have made Achupa understand him; he thought to himself: "Surely she cannot be alone in the forest, there must be more Indians, the best way would be to go for help." But Achupa was a girl of intrepid courage, and the fact was, for the first time, the Indian girl loved, and Arthur Bolton was the object of her devotion. She never expected him to return her love, though Achupa, of a handsome race, was one of the most beautiful of her tribe; but she would sacrifice life to save the white man she secretly loved.

She said to herself "they have killed him," and her eyes flashed, and her bosom heaved, "they shall die;" and drawing an arrow from her quiver—Joe, in the faint light, to his horror beheld her take her bow and creep to within fifteen paces of the mouth of the cave. Achupa fixed her arrow in the bow, and, stood upright, her dark form concealed by the trunk of the tree.

The three Mexicans, after the horrid butchery of their comrade, were coolly cooking their supper at the large fire blazing near the mouth of the cave. Achupa was acknowledged by all the tribe the best shot amongst all the maidens, and even rivaled many of the best amongst the braves. She was strong of arm, and firm of heart.

Before Joe could recover from his amazement at her daring, the arrow sped, with wonderful force; almost the same instant it stuck quivering in the throat of one of the Mexicans, who rolled over on his back, kicking and struggling in the agonies of death. Joe started to his feet. But Achupa pulled him down flat beside herself, for the amazed Mexicans snatched up their muskets, and as Joe, in his awkwardness, snapped some dried branches, they levelled their muskets and fired. Had they been even on their knees, they would have received the balls in their bodies, for they crashed and scattered the twigs and leaves an inch above their heads.

Achupa kept her hand pressed upon Joe's arm, intimating to him not to stir. The Mexicans were now evidently terrified, and afraid to expose themselves; they lifted their comrade, but he was quite dead. They then began to reload their muskets, keeping as much in shelter as possible. Achupa was prepared for another shot, and Joe determined to rush at the remaining one with the spear, provided Achupa wounded another; one of the Mexicans, no doubt thinking that the fire betrayed their movements, moved out from his shelter to disperse the wood embers; as he did so, an arrow pierced him in the side; with a frantic howl of pain the man broke the shaft, and then the two fairly fled, crashing through the branches, and making for their canoe. Achupa and Joe listened, but the tempest was at its height. Neither stirred for a considerable time; but after awhile Achupa crept after the retreating Mexicans, motioning Joe to stay where he was.

She was nearly an hour away; and yet so silently and noiselessly did she return, and her dark form so mingled with the dark objects around, that till she touched him, Joe knew not that she was beside him.

"Come," said the Indian girl—one of the words Arthur Bolton had taught her—"Come," and she walked fearlessly towards the cave. Joe grasping the spear, followed. They entered the cave, and Joe threw some dry wood on the fires, and then gazed anxiously round the cavern. Achupa lighted a pine torch, and then they began searching the cave for our hero and Saunders, whom the Indian girl knew must be imprisoned somewhere in the cavern, for out they did not go.

The light of the torch shewed them the fissure between the rocks, and with an exclamation, Achupa passed through and paused, with an emotion of terror, on the brink of the chasm. Joe's first thought was that the Mexicans had thrown his master and Saunders into the pit. Achupa thought the same, and the young girl trembled; waving her torch, she gazed down its depths, whilst Joe shouted at the top of his voice. Immediately the voice of Arthur Bolton answered from below. The joy of Achupa and Joe was in truth great; Joe jumped about like a madman, and the Indian girl's tears ran down her dark cheeks with joy.

Joe, approaching the mouth of the pit, gazed into it to see if by any possibility he could go down, but Achupa shook her head, and then began to think; but Arthur Bolton called out, telling Joe to make a slight rope of dried grass, full seventy feet long; that he had a strong rope below, which Joe could haul up by the grass cord, and then making it fast, he would then be able to ascend; but that Saunders was lying below, and had just expired.

Joe was amazed; Achupa eagerly listened, and tried to understand from him what his master said. By signs he made her comprehend what he wanted to do. She understood him at once, and then both went into the outer cave. Joe shuddered as he looked upon the dead body of the Mexican desperado—the arrow had pierced the throat through and through. Gathering a quantity of the long jungle grass, Joe began twisting it into a thin line, and Achupa's nimble fingers assisted; between them, in an incredibly short time, they had a line ready of the requisite length, and then, fastening it to a piece of stick, they lowered it down, till the cheerful tones of our hero's voice calling out, "All right," made them pause. Having fastened the strong rope, by which he had been lowered, to the line, they drew it up. The next thing was to fasten it; this was a puzzle—for our hero called out that there was no more rope to spare. So Joe gave it a turn round his own body, and lay down, placing his feet against a projecting rock; he then called out that it was fast.

It required a strong and uncommonly active man to ascend a height of seventy feet by a single, unknotted rope, especially as the sides of the cave had few projections; but the captive was both powerful and active, and in a few minutes he stood panting upon the summit, and seeing the joy of the Indian girl, he caught her in his arms and kissed her cheek, and then rung Joe's hand till his fingers tingled.

"Thank God! thank God! for this deliverance from that fearful hole," he exclaimed, his eyes moistening as he thought of the terrible death he had escaped. He thought he could never repay Achupa, whose bright eyes sparkled with intense pleasure.

"And so, sir, that villain, Saunders, is dead, and down there," said Joe. "How the dickens did he get there?"

"His comrades threw him in, Joe, after lowering me down, and by a most providential circumstance I escaped being crushed to death; but I think I heard the report of guns awhile back—was it so?"

"Yes, sir. I'll tell you all about it by and bye. That brave girl Achupa killed one of the Mexicans with an arrow, and wounded another; they then fired at random and fled, thinking there were many Indians lying hid."

"It is very strange how she came here,"

said Arthur Bolton, and then he made signs with his hands to the Indian girl; she nodded, looked pleased, and then led the way into the outer cave.

"Ah!" said our hero, as the light of the fire fell upon the body of the Mexican, "she is a brave girl. Let us carry this body, Joe, into the inner cave. It's not a pleasant sight; but what a tremendous storm is raging without."

Achupa busied herself, whilst our hero and Joe carried the body of the Mexican away. In hunting about the cavern for food she found the birds Arthur had shot during the day, for the Mexicans had taken them out of the boat and carried them with them for their own use. Achupa, therefore, very calmly replenished the fire, and commenced feathering the teal to make a meal of them. She also found Indian cornmeal in a basket, some plantains, and a couple of gourds full of strong drink.

Neither Bolton nor Joe had tasted food

since the morning, neither had Achupa. Our hero sat down beside her, and endeavoured by all manner of signs and some words he knew of her language, to find out how she came to be alone in the woods. As well as he could make out she explained that she was not alone, that her brother was with her in the morning, but was blown across to the other side of the Punza Pulka river in their small canoe; they came to the wood to set snares for the Indian rabbit and wild ducks. After losing her brother she was making her way to the cave which the Indians frequently retired to when out hunting in those parts, and they had to pass the night there, when she caught sight of the boat with our hero and Joe coming up the creek, and then watched them.

He then contrived by a variety of signs to ask her what became of the other two Mexicans who fled. Achupa replied by signs and words that they fled in their canoe to the other side of the creek.

"Those ruffians will surely return, Joe," said our hero, "when day breaks, to see who killed their comrade. If so we must seize their canoe in order to regain the brig, those aboard will be amazed at our not returning, they will think us swamped by the hurricane."

Aehupa, quite happy at seeing Arthur Bolton released from a frightful death through her means, went on with Joe's assistance roasting the birds for their supper. Our hero strolled outside the cavern to reconnoitre, but the dense darkness of the night, and the furious storm raging drowned every sound, save the crashing of branches and the roar of the gale through the jungle. He considered their situation, without fire-arms to defend themselves, extremely critical. The Mexicans would doubtless get help in a few hours, and return to revenge the death of their comrades, and they had no method of escaping or of regaining the ship in such a tremendous gale of wind as then blew, and one likely at that time of the year to last several days.

Even under the guidance of Achupa it would be difficult to traverse the jungle, swim the creek, and get to the Woolwa Indians. His thoughts then reverted to what he had heard from Saunders, whose recital amazed and excited him. He did not doubt the truth of his words, for his tone and his solemn, subdued, penitent, manner when his last moments approached, removed all shadow of doubt from Arthur's mind that Saunders spoke the truth. According to the dying man's declaration, he believed that he was the son of Sir Richard Morton by his first wife, and that having married again, his father wished the children of his second wife to be his only acknowledged children by the world, and it was evident that it was only lately that the baronet considered him to be his legitimate son, and having found that out had resolved to put him out of the way, at the same time giving him a chance of pushing his fortune in a different part of the world and under another name.

Now what was he to do, presuming his notions to be correct? Was he to force his father to acknowledge him, if disinclined to do so? Where were his proofs of birth—to whom was he to apply for them?

One feeling, however, gave his heart joy; he felt that he was somebody, and he did not despair of getting his father to acknowledge him, he neither coveted his title nor his wealth—simply position. Acknowledged as a member of the Morton family, he would have some hope of gaining the hand of his beloved Alice.

Retiring into the cavern he found supper ready, and the three strangely assorted companions, notwithstanding the perilous scenes they had gone through and might have to go through, set to with very keen appetites to enjoy it. Achupa by signs and words contrived to make Arthur Bolton understand that a watch must be kept all night, and that she would keep awake whilst he and Joe slept.

"No, no!" said our hero, "Joe and I will

watch by turns. You must be fatigued, Achupa."

The Indian maid shook her head and smiled. She could not understand his words, but she knew what he meant, and watch she would; her sense of hearing sounds in the forest was more acute than his, besides, it would be daylight in a few hours.

Arthur Bolton felt that to sleep was out of the question, but, to please Achupa, he stretched himself out by the fire; and Joe, notwithstanding the roar of the storm without the cave, fell asleep in a few moments; and though our hero was kept awake some time by his thoughts, just before daylight he dropped into a profound sleep.

Achupa was a study for a painter, as she paced the cave with noiseless tread, sometimes going without and listening to every sound; her tall and graceful figure became the simple attire she wore, a short petticoat, like a Highlander's kilt, of striped cotton, was fastened round her waist by a belt, ornamented with beads of pure gold; this petticoat was in many folds, gathered to the waist, and reached nearly to the knee; round her left shoulder she wore a scarf, which fastened to the belt round her waist; and on her feet were a pair of very handsome mocassins, lacing up a very beautiful leg. Her skin was very little darker than a Creole's, and her hair was of a beautifully glossy black, and merely confined to the head by a band of hide, ornamented with beads and a small light scarlet feather.

Daylight had just commenced, when some sound without the cavern attracted the girl's attention, though the gale still raged unabated. Approaching the mouth of the cavern, and concealing herself by pressing against the rock, she looked out. After a time, as the light increased, something attracted her attention, for she suddenly ran back into the cavern and awoke our hero; he started up, and so did Joe.

"Come," said the Indian girl, "Mexicans,"

and she pointed to the mouth of the cave, and then led the way to the inner cave. As she did so, the report of a musket was heard, and, at the same moment, a ball splintered several pieces of rock from the side of the cavern, close beside where our hero stood.

"Ah," said he to Joe, "just as I thought; those rascally Mexicans have come back with the daylight—get behind this rock. Only one at a time can pass into the inner cave, and we are sheltered from their shot."

"Faix, it's a bad job, sir, that we have no fire arms."

"I have Saunders' knife," said Bolton. "Run your hand over the dead Mexican, he doubtless has a knife in his belt, and a Mexican knife is not a bad weapon at close quarters."

All three were safe within the inner cave, in which they could not be distinguished, whilst they could see distinctly anyone approaching the outward cave.

Achupa had her bow and eight arrows, as

deadly a weapon, for a near shot, as a clumsy Mexican musket.

Whoever fired the first shot seemed evidently very cautious at shewing himself, for several minutes passed and not a soul was to be seen near the mouth of the cavern. No doubt they were afraid that there might be many Indians concealed within it.

Half an hour passed, and not a soul was seen stirring across the entrance to the cavern. Arthur was getting impatient, when he felt Achupa lay her hand on his arm, and whisper:—

"Come, white man, come."

Her quick eyes had caught the gleam of steel, amidst the low brush wood, a few feet from the cavern's mouth. Our hero soon beheld the cause of Achupa's emotion, for, cautiously coming forth from the thick jungle, he beheld five of the Mexican desperadoes and three Sambos, all armed with muskets.

"The Lord save us!" said Joe, with unconcealed alarm. "The villains will murder us all."

"Keep a stout heart, Joe," said his master, cheerfully. "Only one can pass through this opening between the two rocks, and their bullets cannot touch us. This brave girl shews no fear."

"Oh, be dad," said Joe, courageously, "I'm not afraid to fight, sir, or to die either; the saints in glory will fight for us against such villains."

Achupa, with her bow, and an arrow on the string, stood concealed, but ready to lodge an arrow in the body of the first Mexican or Sambo that dared attempt the passage. Our hero and Joe, with their long, sharp Spanish knives, fit only for close quarters, and to that it was sure to come, also stood prepared for their enemies. Fire arms were useless, as they left no part of their persons visible.

Evidently the enemy knew not what to do; they saw no one to fire at in the outward cave, and the Mexicans knew to force the entrance to the inner cave would surely be the death of him who made the first rush. Still they advanced to the mouth of the cavern, and keeping as little exposed as possible, with their guns ready cocked, they gazed stealthily in. They could not tell how many Indians might be within the inner cavern, neither could they know how many might be within hearing of their muskets in the forest. But a fierce desire, a thirst for vengeance against those within the cavern, whom they readily surmized had released Arthur Bolton from the pit, induced them to risk their lives to be revenged. Therefore, urging the reluctant Sambos forward by threats, and even blows, they made a rush into the cavern, and for the cleft leading into the inner cave, when an arrow from Achupa's bow stood quivering in the breast of one of the Mexicans, who rolled over, mortally wounded, on the ground, whilst, at the same time, our hero drove Achupa's spear into a Sambo's throat, felling him headlong to the ground. Joe was not idle, for, with the thrust of a knife, he drove back another Sambo. This resistance rendered the Mexicans frantic. Retreating they fired their muskets through the cleft, but with no result. At this moment our hero, anxious to obtain the fallen Mexican's musket and pouch, rushed out; he had just seized them when a shot from one of the Mexican's guns struck him on the side of the head, knocking him senseless beside the dead Sambo.

CHAPTER XII.

When recollection and perception returned to our hero, he appeared to awake as from a trance; he felt as if a long period had elapsed, a dreamy kind of stupor overpowered him; but at length, he became conscious of surrounding objects. What he then saw were realities, not visions of a diseased brain.

Opening his eyes one day he looked around him, and became satisfied that he was not dreaming; he perceived he was lying on an Indian couch, upon soft bedding, and that he was in a spacious Indian hut—it was broad daylight, but he was alone—the door of the hut was open, and a refreshing breeze blew into the room, and he felt new life as he inhaled it. At the further end of the hut was another couch, and hanging above it was the bow and quiver, and several other articles he recognized as Achupa's. Whilst endeavouring to bring the past more distinctly to l is confused brain, a shadow darkened the doorway, and then the Indian girl, with a light step entered the hut. Achupa uttered a cry of joy, as her dark eyes met those of our hero, and he exclaimed:

"Ah! it was no vision—Achupa is alive and well!"

The Indian maid was the next instant beside him, and stretching out his arm he drew her towards him, kissing her cheek as a brother would. Achupa gazed at her patient with delight sparkling in her eyes, and then our hero said:

"Where is Joe?"

Achupa understood the word Joe; but before she could answer him, Joe himself, hearty and well, entered the hut.

Joe's joy was great, seeing his master at last sensible, and able to talk and to know those about him.

Achupa seeing him so well, and anxious to talk to Joe, left the hut to get him food, now that he seemed capable of eating some.

"How long, Joe," questioned our hero, "have I been lying here in this state? I feel all of a sudden quite well. I am certain, for several days back, I have seen you and Achupa and some tall woman, pass before me; but I felt as if I was dreaming, and that you were visions."

"The Lord be praised! sir, that your senses have come back; Achupa said, the last few days, that you were getting round fast, and that you would soon know us again."

"How many days have I been ill, and where am I?"

"Faix, sir, it's just twenty-one days since we came to this village."

"Twenty-one days," repeated our hero, amazed.

"Be dad, it is a fact, sir; you were a week without opening your eyes, and dickens a bit did you eat, all you took was a little liquid Achupa gave you, through a great quill. Punka Pigwash used to shake his head, and sit looking at you, smoking his pipe. 'Be gor,' says he, 'he'll never go to the hunting grounds again, he's done for, and more's the pity;' but Achupa got angry, when he wanted some wise old woman, as thin as a herring, and with a nose like a turnspit, to doctor you her way, and faix, a queer way that was. Be dad, I was going to duck the old witch, she wanted you to be stript and sewed up in the fresh skin of that big beast they call a manitou, and to drink its blood mixed with the oil of a fish's liver and—"

"Confound the old woman," interrupted Arthur Bolton; "a nice way of curing a gunshot wound in the head."

"Bedad, it was if you knew the rest of the doctorings. But, Achupa said she would cure you herself, and thanks to the saints, she has, only using herbs, and washing the wound many times a day. How do you feel your head now, sir?"

"I feel my thoughts and ideas and memory all right, but I cannot move my head without some pain, and I am tired to death lying here."

"A few days more, sir, will set you all right, I hope."

"But, Joe, what must they think aboard the Foam; have you sent any message there, or have they made any enquiries? But first of all, tell me how we were rescued? I remember being hit and falling senseless on the ground. What happened after that?"

"When you fell, sir, Achupa gave a great shriek, for one of those murderous Mexicans was going to run his long knife into you. We both rushed out, and Achupa drove the spear you dropt into the rascal, and then fell on your body, whilst I got a blow on the head that tumbled me over. In two minutes they would have cut all our throats, but there came such a war whoop from the jungle outside that the Mexicans were startled, and before they could escape or do anything, our old friend Bogwash and a dozen Indians rushed in, and in a twinkling they settled the remaining Mexicans, and then pitched the entire dead down the pit to rot with their old comrade Saunders. I saw it all, for though I was knocked down I was sensible enough; and, faix, the Woolwa young gentlemen made very short work of it, they hated the Mexicans so. But I'm sure I'm talking too much, you'll be tired out."

"No, no; excepting a slight heaviness in the head, I feel all right. I owe that kind, noble-hearted Indian girl my life."

"Faix you do, sir, for that respectable old witch would have settled you in no time. But there are letters for you from Bluefields, sir. Messengers have been sent to Bosswash to enquire after you, for the brig has sailed with all the family for Jamaica, and they have left all our things at Bluefields, with the English gentleman who resides there."

"Ah!" said our hero, a little uneasy, "I thought when you said I had been three weeks lying here that such would be the case. No doubt they were all anxious to quit this unhealthy and inhospitable shore. Where is the Indian chief now?"

"The whole tribe are gone on a great hunting expedition, sir; only the squaws and the children remaining."

"I will not read the letters to-day," said Arthur Bolton, "my head would not bear it; but a few days, please God, will enable me to get up."

A week elapsed, however, before he could leave his bed and take air and exercise. Joe replaced Aehupa, watching him at night, and every attention the devoted girl could shew him he received. He rapidly regained strength, and the wound, some small pieces of bone having worked out, became healed, so that a few days more would restore him.

Though health and strength were returning, Arthur Bolton was sad and thoughtful in mind. He had read the three letters sent to him. One of them informed him that when his residence with the Woolwa Indians became known to Mr. and Mrs. Marchmont, Captain Courtney had not entered the harbour of Bluefields with the Foam, she drew too much water, and the gales of wind off the coast were heavy. So he sailed at once for Jamaica, Mr. and Mrs. Marchmont following in a few days with their daughter in the schooner. All our hero's effects were landed from the Foam, and left under the care of Mr. Stockwell, the English resident, with a letter from Captain Courtney to be given him when he reached Bluefields.

One of the letters sent to our hero from Bluefields was from Mr. Marchmont, the other from Mrs. Marchmont, enclosing one from his beloved Alice. This last letter, which he treasured in his heart, consoled him for the somewhat unexpected one he received from Mr. Marchmont. We will give that gentleman's letter in full:

"Bluefields, 184—.

"My Dear Sir,

"We hear with great regret that you are suffering much from a gunshot wound, inflicted by one of those miscreants from whom you rescued my youngest daughter. I would I could send a surgeon to you, but unhappily no such person is to be had here. But we understand you are going on most favorably, and we trust in a very short time that your health will be fully established. Mrs. Marchmont, myself, and daughter, beg to express our most heartfelt gratitude for your most gallant and successful undertaking, risking your life to preserve my youngest daughter. I am quite aware, from Mrs. Marchmont's knowledge of your disposition and character, that an offer of pecuniary recompense would be offensive to your feelings. She has also candidly informed me that during the voyage you entertained an affection for my daughter Alice. Knowing such to be the case and my daughter being very young, and also knowing my views respecting the future settlement of my daughters, Mrs. Marchmont has acted very imprudently and weakly in not at once checking an intimacy that could only lead to unpleasant results.

"From what I have heard of your character and conduct, I could have no possible objection to receiving you as a suitor for my daughter, provided you had a name and position in the world; I could dispense with wealth, but never the want of birth and position. God forbid I should say this to wound your feelings in the slightest degree, for I esteem and admire your principles and your conduct. But you are young, and so slight an attachment as one contracted in a few weeks at sea may easily be conquered, and I trust your own good sense will convince you that I am not harsh or unfeeling to you. We shall return immediately to England. I shall abandon my intention of remaining in Jamaica a year or so, and I now offer you, if you are willing to accept it, one of the most lucrative situations for a young man on the island.

"You will begin with a salary of £400 a year. I will leave full instructions with my agent in Jamaica, Mr. Fitzhugh, a gentleman of high integrity and in a most responsible position. He will make you fully acquainted with the situation I trust you will accept, and I sincerely hope we shall meet in a few years without any feeling on your part that I have acted ungenerously or harshly, after the great service my family have experienced at your hands. Wishing you a speedy restoration to health, and a prosperous career,

"I remain,

"Ever gratefully yours,

"PHILIP ARCHIBALD MARCHMONT."

Mrs. Marchmont's letter was all a noble fond mother could write. She bade the deliverer of her child from a cruel fate never despair. She earnestly implored him to accept the situation her husband earnestly wished him to fill, and to trust to her endeavours and time, to bring Mr. Marchmont round to her views. As to her daughter, though she would never disobey her father by marrying without his consent, still her heart was firmly and irrevocably his, and no other should ever possess her hand. It was a long letter, full of motherly feeling, and motherly counsel, and it soothed and calmed the irritation of feeling he certainly felt on perusing Mr. Marchmont's epistle.

Alice's fond and most feeling letter he treasured in his heart of hearts. She was herself not without hope. She said her father was a most loving, kind parent, and one that would never force her inclinations, though he refused his consent to their union. Alice did not appear to wish him to accept the situation offered him in Jamaica. She wished him to exert all his energies in investigating the mystery that enveloped his origin, and this wish Arthur Bolton resolved to follow up, especially after hearing William Saunders's declaration, and get to England on the first opportunity.

As for Achupa, content at beholding Arthur Bolton's restoration to health, in accompanying him and Joseph and some of the tribe on short hunting excursions, her days passed quite happily, without bestowing a thought upon the time when the white men should leave her presence for ever.

Punka Bosswash had returned after a most successful hunting expedition, and was heartily rejoiced to see our hero restored to his former vigour.

He had concluded a peace with the Sambos of Quamwatta, who, now that the Mexican desperadoes were exterminated, very willingly agreed to his proposals. They were no longer to be opposed when inclined to capture turtle, and no amount of shells was to be payed for permission to frequent the turtle grounds, and in return for these concessions, they were to supply the Sambos with the game of their forests—for the Sambos were but poor hunters—in exchange for other commodities.

Mr. Marchmont, before leaving Bluefields, sent Punka Bosswash many presents, amongst them a dozen excellent muskets with a considerable amount of ammunition. To Achupa both mother and daughter sent many pretty trinkets and ornaments, so that the chief and his tribe were quite proud of the part they had played in the rescue of Mr. Marchmont's daughter, and of Arthur Bolton.

Achupa, when our hero told her of his intended departure, appeared to realize her feelings, and to feel acutely what the separation would cost her. Arthur always treated the Indian girl with most affectionate, brotherly tenderness; he had taught her, during his three months' residence with the tribe, to speak and understand many English words, and he had himself picked up almost enough of her language to ask for anything he wanted. The young Indians of the tribe looked upon him with most favorable eyes;

he brought down his game with his rifle, with unerring eye; he could match the best amongst them in activity, and in strength he surpassed them. They all, therefore, looked upon his departure with exceeding regret, and half-a-dozen of the youths of the tribe were selected to take him and Joe to Bluefields, and a fine, roomy canoe having been prepared, they were to descend the Punza Pulka river and then coast it to the Bluefields lagoon.

Achupa bore the departure of her favorite with apparent fortitude; at least no one present could judge of her feelings of bitter regret by her features or manner.

She called to her aid all the wonderful fortitude and stoical indifference an Indian can command, under every trial, whether torture of body or mind.

Arthur, who twice owed his life to the courage and fidelity of the chief's daughter, felt and shewed his affection and gratitude by his manner, and told the young girl that he should never forget her, and kissed and bade her farewell with all the natural affection of a brother. He had no token of remembrance to leave her, but her brother, who was to accompany him to Bluefields, he promised should bring her one. As our hero entered the canoe, and it paddled down the creek, Achupa turned away with a swelling heart and sought the deep solitude of the forest. Of the after-fate or life of the Indian girl we know nothing, as Arthur Bolton never set foot on the Musquito shore again after leaving it, during the remainder of his life.

The party reached Bluefields in safety. Mr. Stockwell received our hero kindly, and offered him every hospitality in his power. From his private effects, Arthur selected the only valuable article he possessed—the gold chain of his watch—for Achupa, which he begged her brother to give her, with his most affectionate regards. To the six Indians he gave each a musket and pistol, which he purchased from Mr. Stockwell's store, together with some ammunition. The delighted Indians bade him farewell with great regret, and returned at once to their tribe, quite proud of their presents, which they fired several times in imitation of the English war schooner when saluting the Governor.

By great good fortune an American brig touched at Bluefields, bound to Liverpool, and in her our hero took his passage—leaving several letters with Mr. Stockwell to forward by the first vessel to Jamaica. In his letter to Mr. Marchmont, he thanked him for his offer of a situation, but simply stated that circumstances had occurred which prevented his accepting so lucrative a post, and that he was about to return to England by the first opportunity that offered. To Mrs. Marchmont he expressed all he felt; he declared that his devotion to Alice would only cease with life, and that he did not despair of proving himself worthy of her love and her hand. He said nothing about his hopes of discovering the mystery of his birth, or of the revelations made to him by William Saunders; he would not raise hopes in his beloved Alice's heart that might never be realized. Satisfied with the knowledge of her faith and undying love, he left his intention unrevealed. But our hero might as well not have written, for before his letter reached Jamaica Mr. Marchmont's family had sailed for England.

Our hero and Joe, after a prosperous voyage, reached Liverpool on the 9th of October, just fourteen days after the landing of the Marchmont family at Southampton. They had returned to England with Captain Courtney in the Foam.

Establishing himself at the Blue Boar Hotel, Liverpool, his first object was to fit himself and Joe out, for their stock of garments required replenishing. He possessed in reality but a small sum, but he retained the order of £100 from a London Bank upon a mercantile firm in Jamaica, and he made no doubt but that the bank would pay the amount, as it was expressly payable to himself. Therefore, having provided himself with suitable garments, he took the train to London. The following day he presented himself at the Banking Establishment of Messrs. Freeman and James.

Requesting to see either of the partners, he was shown into a private room, where sat Mr. James, busy with his ledgers and accounts.

"I presume, Sir," said our hero, after taking a chair, "you recognize this document; it was intended to be presented by me to a firm in Jamaica, but circumstances prevented my reaching that place. I suppose the order is presentable here."

Mr. James took the paper and read it over, then looked up and regarded our hero attentively for a moment, said: "I remember this order very well, sir. The sum was lodged in our hands, and we gave this order payable to Mr. Arthur Bolton to a highly respectable firm in Jamaica. You are Mr. Bolton I presume." On our hero answering in the affirmative, Mr. James continued: "Can you bring any resident in London to testify to your being the proper person named in this order, for if my memory does not fail me, I saw some time back, how many months ago I cannot say, a reward offered by a Superintendent of Police for any information respecting the disappearance of a gentleman named Arthur Bolton, from the Crown Hotel. The name struck me at the time, but as Arthur Bolton is not at all an uncommon name, I did not, after a moment's thought, connect the name with that in the order, as the person who obtained it was a gentleman of rank, wealth, and station, in fact Sir Richard Morton, of Morton Manor, Derbyshire, who said he required it for a young man who was going out to the West Indies to fill a lucrative situation. Now, are you the Mr. Bolton advertised for? or are you the Mr. Bolton, who—"

"One and the same person, Mr. James," interrupted our hero, smiling, "and the Superintendent of Police you mention, if in London, will at once identify me as the Arthur Bolton missing, for any information concerning whom he advertised."

"Still," said the careful Mr. James, a little mystified, "that will not make you out the Arthur Bolton to whom this order is payable. You will pardon me, I do not in the least doubt your word, still it is absolutely necessary that—"

Mr. James was interrupted by a slight knock at the door, and a gentleman entered the room; he was a tall, handsome man, scarcely fifty. The moment the stranger entered, Mr. James jumped up, and as he heartily shook hands with him, he said: "You have taken me by surprise; by jove, you look well and hearty. I saw your arrival in the paper a few days ago. How have you left Mrs. Marchmont and your daughters."

Arthur Bolton gave such a start at the name of Marchmont, that he upset his chair, which caused Mr. James to turn round. Looking surprized at our hero, whose agitation was perceptible, he said: "If Mr. Bolton, you—" here the worthy banker paused, for the start his friend Mr. Marchmont gave at the name of Bolton was quite as great, and his agitation was also as perceptible as our hero's.

Mr. Marchmont, to do him justice, though a proud man, and an ambitious man, was a gentleman of highly honourable principles, and generous to a degree. He recovered himself first, and to the intense surprise of the banker, advanced towards our hero, and holding out his hand, said:

"You must be the Mr. Arthur Bolton to whom myself and family are under such weighty obligations; my wife's description of you is too correct to be mistaken."

"This meeting is very strange, Mr. Marchmont," said our hero, much pleased with the manner and appearance of Alice's father—"for I believed you still in Jamaica. My letter, in reply to your generous proposals, I forwarded from Bluefields to Jamaica; of course you never received it."

"No," returned Mr. Marchmont, "we left the island before it arrived there. But all this is a mystery to you, friend James," continued Mr. Marchmont, turning to the banker.

"By Jove, you are right, Marchmont; but in one thing I am quite satisfied, that I now require no further proof of this gentleman's being the person he represents himself."

"Oh, I'll answer for that," said Mr. Marchmont, "though this is the first time we ever met. However, as we must not occupy your valuable time, friend James, I must beg Mr. Bolton to favour me with his company at dinner. I am at the Clarendon, all alone, for my family will remain some time at Southampton."

Our hero willingly and gladly accepted the invitation, and Mr. James, signing the order for the £100, which he told him he would receive in the office, took leave of both gentlemen, received his money, and returned well satisfied to his hotel, where he found Joseph transformed into a very smart, handsome lad, as an attendant, having had a complete outfit.

Joe was so attached to our hero, and he to him, having gone through such perilous scenes together, that he could not bear to part with him, and as he determined to share his fortunes, whether good or bad, and had neither parents nor relatives that he knew of, our hero gladly consented.

After Arthur's departure from the banker's, Mr. James, an old and very esteemed friend of Mr. Marchmont's, said:

"That is a remarkably fine young fellow that has just left us. Confess now, is there not some mystery about him? Though you seem never to have met, yet you deem yourself under great obligation to him."

"So I am," returned Mr. Marchmont. "I'll dine with you to-morrow, and tell you all about him. There is some mystery about his birth; in fact, he knows nothing respecting his parentage."

"Nevertheless," said the Banker, thoughtfully, "I could give a very good guess as to who his father is."

"The deuce you can, James. How have you got a glimpse into the past history of this young man? Tell me, for though I am come on business, I feel so deep an anxiety concerning that young man, that anything you can tell me I shall be grateful for."

"Well, the fact is, friend, I believe him to be the illegitimate son of Sir Richard Morton, of Morton Manor, Derbyshire."

Mr. Marchmont's cheek flushed; he did not like this announcement. The bar-sinister was a terrible bar to jump over, if ever he entertained the prospect of bestowing his daughter's hand upon her deliverer; for Mr. Marchmont had very clearly seen that his daughter's attachment to Arthur Bolton was no evanescent feeling to be cast off at pleasure.

"Why do you think so, James?" he demanded of the banker.

"Well, I will tell you. Our bank has large dealings with the Morton family. They are now abroad. It was only the other day I remitted them a letter on a Geneva Bank. Sir Richard Morton is married to a younger daughter of the late Lord Pintire—a good match in every way—and has a son and two daughters grown up; the son and heir is about nineteen. Sir Richard came to me some months ago, faith, nearly a year ago, and told me he wanted to send a young man he took a great interest in, out to Jamaica, to pursue a mercantile career, and begged me to give him a letter of introduction to a respectable merchant at Kingstown, and a letter of credit upon a banking firm there, for £100, for his private purse, till he got employment. He told me he was a highly-educated youth, about twenty-two.

"Humph!" said I to myself. "Twenty-two years of age. Very likely to be his own son. Sir Richard has the character of having been wild and extravagant in his youth, and there were some queer stories afloat, I heard them myself, when in that part of the country. However, I said nothing on the subject, gave him the order on a firm you know very well, and also a letter to the principal partner, that would be sure to get his protegé a first-rate situation out there."

"Ah!" said Mr. Marchmont, "after all, you only surmise, or think it likely he is Sir Richard Morton's son."

"Of course, my dear friend, I cannot speak positively, but I remember about that time an advertisement appeared in several papers, that somehow attracted my attention. The exact particulars I cannot give you, but it had reference to the singular disappearance of a young gentleman of the name of Arthur Bolton, who was known to have left the Crown Hotel, Cavendish Square, to visit some house in a low locality, near London bridge. From the time he left the Hotel nothing further was heard of him; his trunk, &c., remained in the Hotel, and for any information respecting the said Arthur Bolton, a considerable reward was offered."

"This is somewhat mysterious and extraordinary," remarked Mr. Marchmont, "and quite out of our power at present to unravel. To-morrow, however, I shall be able to understand matters more clearly, for I expect to learn everything concerning him that he himself can impart."

The two gentlemen then proceeded to talk upon business matters, and after a time Mr. Marchmont took leave of his friend, the banker.

CHAPTER XIII.

On arriving in London our hero avoided taking up his abode in the Crown Hotel, where he had left his luggage, and from which he had so mysteriously disappeared. He wished to remain quiet and unnoticed, and disliked becoming an object of curiosity, at all events for the present. Full of hope and happy anticipations of the future, he proceeded to dine with Mr. Marchmont, who received him in the most cordial manner, and whose conversation during dinner was varied and agreeable, insensibly leading his young guest to speak on various subjects, and thus discovering how well he had profited by the education he had received, and how capable he was of succeeding in any career fortune might place before him. It was not till after the meal was ended, and as they sat over their wine, that Mr. Marchmont said—

"Before, my dear young friend, I ask you a few questions, I must inform you that since we left Jamaica my mind has been completely changed on one point. I mention it now, that hereafter, should circumstances turn out favourable to your hopes, you may not suppose me influenced by those circumstances."

Arthur listened with wrapt attention and considerable emotion as Mr. Marchmont continued—

"When I first heard from my wife of the mutual attachment between you and Alice, I confess I was much annoyed. I gave you in my letter my reasons for feeling so, therefore it is unnecessary to repeat them. Since then I have thought much on the subject, studied my daughter's character, considered the services you had rendered her, and the likelihood of a very strong attachment arising out of the circumstances in which you both were placed; therefore I was prepared, when I encountered you so singularly at my old college friend and correspondent, Mr. James's, to feel very favourably disposed towards you, and I did intend to write to you—thinking you still in Jamaica—to that effect. My short acquaintance with you has strengthened my determination, and I now tell you whether you succeed in ascertaining who your parents were or not, it will make no difference in my wish to consider you as my future son-in-law."

Arthur sprang from his chair, his face flushed with excitement, and his heart beating almost painfully with joy and happiness; grasping Mr. Marchmont's hand, he expressed himself so well, and painted the happiness he experienced so eloquently, that that gentleman himself became exceedingly moved, and embraced our hero with a great deal of affection in his manner.

After a few moments they became more

composed, and Mr. Marchmont then requested to be told every particular connected with his infancy and manhood.

All was quickly related, and the dying declaration of William Saunders astonished Mr. Marchmont much, as he emphatically declared—

"There must be some foundation for this man's statement; but allowing its perfect truth, there will be immense difficulties to contend with. Sir Richard Morton will, no doubt endeavour to maintain the legality of his present wife's children's claim to the title and estates. I do not see how you can proceed without the evidence of that man Reynolds, or rather Mason. I would advise you to try and see Mr. Baldwin, the Superintendent of Police to-morrow; it strikes me that he meant more in the advertisements he put in the papers at the time of your disappearance than meets the eye. In two or three days I shall be ready to accompany you into Hampshire, where all, I need not say, will be rejoiced to see you. I shall write to-morrow."

After passing one of the happiest evenings of his life, our hero bade Mr. Marchmont good night, and returned to his hotel, to indulge in golden dreams, whenever his happy anticipations of soon seeing Alice allowed him to close his eyes in sleep.

Whilst eating his breakfast the following morning he took up a morning paper, and in turning it over carelessly his gaze rested upon a heading of a column in large characters—as follows:

"MYSTERIOUS MURDER OF AN ENGLISH BARONET IN AMERICA."

The young man felt a strange feeling of dread steal over him as he perused those words, but he read on—

"It is with exceeding pain and regret that we have to record the violent death of an English baronet, of station and fortune, Sir Richard Morton."

A pang shot through the reader's frame, and for a moment a mist was before his eyes, and the hand that held the paper trembled as he murmured:

"My God! my father! I know it, I feel he was my father."

Whilst he remained in a manner overpowered, the door opened and Mr. Marchmont hastily entered the room. He, too, was agitated as he said, taking a chair:

"I see you have read this dreadful news, Arthur; it is horrible!"

"Horrible!" repeated our hero; "yes, it's a horrible crime, and to me it's a fearful blow. I know he was my father, be it how it may; and now I shall never feel the embrace of a parent, and I trusted, hoped, prayed, that things would so turn out, that at least he would acknowledge me as his son and give me his blessing," and Arthur Bolton shewed that he was deeply moved.

"I feel for you indeed, my dear Arthur," said Mr. Marchmont, taking a paper from his pocket; "it will be a terrible blow to the bereaved Lady Morton's family. But have you read the article? It's exceedingly strange Sir Richard Morton's going to America, and it's still more strange, the terrible events hinted at in this article, that took place before the baronet and his family left England."

"I have not read it, my dear sir. I was so shocked when I came to Sir Richard Morton's name that I read no further."

"I will read the statement in this paper; it has a much longer and apparently clearer article than the paper you were perusing."

Mr. Marchmont then read as follows:

"About this period last year we mentioned in our columns an occurrence that took place in the family of Sir Richard Morton, of Morton Chase, Derbyshire, which created considerable excitement at that time in the vicinity.

"One morning Sir Richard was found by Lady Morton in his library, apparently bleeding to death from the stab of a bowie knife, lying on the floor beside him. Most fortunately a surgeon, coming to visit one of the servants of the family, was riding up the avenue, and most probably Sir Richard Morton's life was saved by his prompt assistance. Still he was in great peril. An eminent physician from the metropolis was sent for, and after a long and painful illness the baronet recovered. All that the public ever knew of this mysterious attempt at assassination was, that a person had requested to see Sir Richard that morning, and was shown into the library where the baronet was. An hour or so afterwards he was seen to leave the house, and Lady Morton going to the library found her husband insensible. When Sir Richard recovered sufficiently, the whole family proceeded to pass the winter in a mild climate.

" So far these circumstances were forgotten by the general public, when the startling intelligence of the unfortunate Sir Richard Morton's murder reached England. The first intimation was copied from a New York paper, but we have now authentic particulars from our own reporter. It appears that the baronet was in Delawarr on business, that he visited a farm house called the Fork, and that the owner of Fork farm, it has been ascertained was formerly in Sir Richard's employment as bailiff at Morton Chase. This man's name was Mason."

"Ah!" interrupted our hero. "Mason, that's the real name of the man who enticed me into the house in Thames Street, and afterwards put me on board the Foam."

"Yes," returned Mr. Marchmont, "I remember; there is some terrible mystery connected with that family of Mason. I am convinced with them lies the elucidation of the mystery of your birth. I will continue the paragraph."

"It seems Sir Richard Morton, and an attorney named Bowen, had an interview with Mr. Mason in Delawarr, and that Mason signed some important papers and documents, which the deceased baronet wished to bring safely to England, and for that purpose carried them on his person. He left Delawarr attended by a guide, both on horseback. In passing through a wood, about ten or twelve miles from Delawarr, the guide, riding in advance, heard the report of a gun, and turning round beheld the unfortunate baronet fall from his horse, evidently killed, for he never stirred after reaching the ground. The guide was terrified, and whilst he hesitated, a ball whistled close to his own ear, which made him put his horse to a gallop. He fled to a small road side inn about three miles off to procure help.

"When Sir Richard's body was found and conveyed to Delawarr, Mr. Bowen the attorney was sent for. He ordered that an instant investigation might be made of the deceased's garments for the papers, but neither papers, money, watch, or even the ring on the finger —a very valuable one—were found; all had been abstracted before those who found the body reached the spot. I am prevented," continued the reporter, "giving you further particulars, as I have only ten minutes in which to finish my letter. By next mail I shall, I trust, be able to throw some light upon this mysterious and horrible crime."

"This fearful act has been committed, I feel fully satisfied," said Arthur, deeply affected, "by those Masons, to get possession of those papers, for what use or purpose, I can only imagine. I will leave England, for America by the very next packet, and never cease till I discover the miserable wretches who committed this crime, and bring them to justice."

"I think you are right, Arthur," replied Mr. Marchmont. "The next packet sails from Southampton on the 18th, this is the 12th. I will be ready to leave London with you on the 14th, and will see you off; before which, try and find Mr. Baldwin, the Superintendent of Police, he may be able to give you information that may be useful."

After some further discussion upon the late event, and the manner in which our hero would act on reaching Delawarr, they separated, Arthur proceeding to the station, to enquire after the Superintendent of Police.

Mr. Baldwin had arrived the day before from Canterbury, and was, when our hero enquired for him, in his office.

He recognized Arthur at once, but his surprise was very great, as he sprang from his seat, and shook him warmly by the hand, saying:

"This is a surprise, indeed. If you disappeared mysteriously, your return is quite as singular. I sincerely rejoice to see you alive and well, but this is no place for us to converse in, we shall be interrupted every moment, as I have one or two cases to dispose of."

"Well then, my dear sir, can you make it convenient to dine with me at the Clarendon, name your own hour; I have a great deal to say to you."

"Well, be it so," returned the Superintendent. "Say seven o'clock, and I will be with you, for I have important matter to communicate."

"Seven o'clock it shall be," said our hero, and shaking hands with the kind hearted Mr. Baldwin, he left the office.

Mr. Baldwin was punctual to the hour appointed, and they sat down to dinner, during which the conversation turned on indifferent subjects. When the wine and dessert were placed upon the table, and they were left to themselves, Mr. Baldwin, who was exceedingly anxious to hear our hero's adventures, begged him to give him a brief outline of them.

Arthur did so; the worthy Superintendent listened, exceedingly astonished.

"You have been quite a hero of romance," he remarked, "and your life has been preserved in a most providential manner. Your narrative satisfies me," continued the Superintendent, "that my conjectures respecting your birth, were, from the beginning, nearly correct. The mysterious murder of your father,

Sir Richard Morton, is a terrible blow, for I feel convinced his proceeding to America was for the express purpose of restoring you to your rightful position as his son and heir, and I am also satisfied that the Masons were the perpetrators of the horrid crime related in the papers."

"Yes," said our hero, with a sigh of deep regret, "of that I am sure; but I wish, before I leave, to gain all the information I can respecting the Masons, previous to their leaving England."

"I can give you every information you require," returned Mr. Baldwin, "and also inform you of some parts of your family history unknown to you. I dare say you have often wondered how Mrs. Morton, of Ramsgate, came to be so completely separated from all intercourse with her family?"

"Yes," replied Arthur, "I have often thought of that."

"Mrs. Morton," continued Mr. Baldwin, "was, you know, many years older than her brother, Sir Richard. During her father's life, she ran away with a man every way inferior to herself in birth and position. She got married, and went on the Continent. The man, whose name was Polson, was a low bred adventurer, and finding he could not make it up with your grandfather, who sternly refused to give his daughter one shilling, took to drinking and gaming, and was finally consigned to a Neapolitan prison, for swindling and stabbing a Neapolitan officer. The officer did not die, and after a certain term of imprisonment, Polson would have been released, but before that time, he, with five criminals, attempted an escape, and was shot dead by one of the jailers they had nearly murdered. It was a good riddance, however, but Mrs. Polson, broken hearted, and feeling her degradation terribly, returned penniless to England. There she learned her father's death, and feeling no desire to visit her native place, she wrote to Sir Richard, describing her situation, and stating her determination to drop her husband's name, and return to some town in England, where, under the name of Mrs. Morton, she could live in great retirement, if a small annuity were allowed her. Sir Richard settled on her £500 a year (she in reality being entitled to the sum of £10,000), provided she continued single, and lived in retirement. After a while she settled in Ramsgate, and there she remained till her death. All this I discovered during my enquiries after you.

"When you disappeared so suddenly from the Crown Hotel, I set a most intelligent officer on your track, and also inserted an advertisement in the daily papers.

"The officer I employed tracked the two men who decoyed you to the old house in Thames Street into Derbyshire, and with a comrade, by my permission, pursued and tracked them into the vicinity of Morton Chase; then it was that this Reynolds or Mason attempted to assassinate Sir Richard Morton. By a concatination of untoward circumstances, Mason and Saunders baffled the detectives, and finally got off in a vessel to America.

"I was desperately vexed, and some short time after, having a week to spare, I went myself into Derbyshire, where I was quite unknown, and took up my abode at the little inn in which my two detectives had been baffled, after actually having Mason and Saunders in their power. Sir Richard and family had at this time left the country for the Continent. Of course the recent attempt at assassination, and the escape of the criminal formed a fertile source of conversation all over that neighbourhood. Knowing Reynolds' real name to be Mason, I began my investigations. I learned that the mother of the woman who kept the little inn had once been a servant of John Mason's when a bailiff on the estate of Morton Chase. She was then a very old woman, and was living with her son, a joiner at Chatsworth.

"Well, I went to Chatsworth, and found

James Dulford, the joiner, and the mother; they were both very shy in answering any questions, and I despaired of gaining any information, till I found out that James Dulford was in difficulties, and was sued for a sum of £30.

"He was about to sell off all he possessed, and put his mother in the poor-house, when I stepped in and offered to pay off his debts, provided his mother would give me truthful answers to a few questions I wished to ask her. The old woman was awfully afraid of the workhouse, and she said—

"'I know very well what you wish to know, and I can tell things worth hundreds to the right person; but I'm told he's dead.'

"'Well, there's the £30,' said I, putting three ten pound notes on the table, 'and I promise you this, if the person you mean is not dead—and I am pretty certain he is not—you shall get well rewarded for any information you may give me.'

"'Well, indeed, sir, I fear he has been

made away with,' said the old dame, 'and I will tell you why I think so. I saw George Mason, not six weeks ago, and he said, in talking about him, "He's dead by this time, at all events." Now why he should wish him dead, I cannot imagine.'

"Do you know, my young friend," continued the Superintendent, "that I was really startled by what the old woman said, for I began to imagine Mason and his accomplice might have been excited by any resistance you were sure to offer, to kill you, though what benefit they could gain, like the old woman, I could not imagine."

"Ah!" observed our hero, "I now see where I committed a great error. When the Foam lay to off Ramsgate to take up passengers, I ought to have written you a line, and explained how I had been carried off. Your kindness and interest in my affairs I can never sufficiently appreciate, and your expenses—"

"Oh, we will talk upon that subject hereafter, my dear sir; we have some difficulties to overcome yet. If you fail to recover those most important papers, so mysteriously taken from the baronet's person at the time of his death, we shall, I fear, be baffled by the technicalities of the law. I can make it quite clear to the understanding, and to the public in general that you are unquestionably Sir Richard Morton's eldest legitimate son; but the law, to substantiate your claim will require something more than assertions. Let me give you the substance of the intelligence I was able to obtain from old Dame Dulford. By her account she lived as domestic servant with the Masons several years before the late baronet came into possession of the Morton estates. It is necessary, though painful, to state that your father, before he came into possession of the estates, had actually courted, and even talked of marriage, to John Mason's eldest daughter; whose father had great hopes of being able to entrap the young baronet, when he came of age, into a marriage; but at this time there came on a visit to the Masons a schoolfellow, an orphan, and extremely beautiful. Miss Grace Manning, by a strange freak of nature, bore an extraordinary resemblance to old Mason's daughter. When not together they were singularly likely to be mistaken for each other. But they were widely different in temper and disposition. The young baronet transferred his attentions and affections to Grace Manning. It was at this period that Sir Richard Morton discovered that John Mason had put his signature to a £1,000 cheque. He thus gained complete power over the Masons, and, I regret to say, he forced them to aid his designs upon Grace Manning. A false marriage was intended, but John Mason, to be revenged, to a certain extent, upon the baronet, employed a real clergyman, but a most consummate rascal, a disgrace to the cloth, and who shortly after met his deserts, was disgraced, and had to fly the country to avoid prosecution for fraud. Your poor mother, who was, Mrs. Dulford said, devotedly attached to your father, fortunately never knew the fraud her husband intended her; she died in giving you birth. The Masons knew that they had Sir Richard Morton in their power, for a year after his wife's death he married again, a lady of station and fortune, who was devotedly attached to him. Old Mrs. Dulford acknowledged to me she knew that Jay Pearson was a clergyman, and that she received ten pounds for keeping the secret. But it seems that this same Jay Pearson departed without giving them the certificate of the marriage, and before John Mason could get hold of him, he had fled to America. The whole proceedings of the Masons before their departure for America was a deep-laid scheme, to hold Sir Richard Morton in perpetual terror, and by those means extort money. The only mystery I cannot well understand was the attempt to assassinate Sir Richard Morton in his library. Nor could Mrs. Dulford enlighten me on that particular subject, although she hid George

Mason in her house for three days after his flight from Morton Chase, and finally aided him in escaping out of the country, by disguising him in female apparel."

"I have no doubt," remarked Arthur, "that my father proceeded to America, for the sole purpose of unravelling the mystery of his first marriage, and to obtain positive information relative to my mother's death, information so important, for without such proof his second marriage became a myth, and his children illegitimate; a circumstance sufficient to break his heart, or render the remainder of his days wretched."

"Happily," remarked Mr. Baldwin, "Lady Morton and her children are saved from such an infliction, and though you would, of course, take the title and family estates, yet Lady Morton's own large fortune, settled on herself, and an estate worth £1,500 a year, left her eldest son by an uncle, leaves them not only independent, but affluent. The great question is to gain possession of the stolen papers

—stolen, no doubt, for the sake of the reward that may be offered. There will be no difficulty in proving that you are the infant abandoned on the sands at Ramsgate, the chain of evidence on that point is clear and decisive."

END OF VOL. II.

CPSIA information can be obtained
at www.ICGtesting.com
Printed in the USA
LVHW042143040522
717863LV00005B/290

9 783375 002527